"What Are You Afraid of, Tom?"

"Involvement."

"With me?" She stiffened. "Because of my family?"

"No!" He was close and warm. "Oh, Serena, it's happening again. It's something I can't seem to control. I want you so . . ."

"We can't, Tom. It's not good for either of us." But her hands longed to touch him, and her words echoed against his lips.

"What if we were to pretend," Tom began, breathing raggedly, "that we had no past? That we were two different people? That we were . . . in love . . . ?"

BILLIE DOUGLASS

enjoys writing romances and confesses that her "family, friends, and imagination" influence what ultimately comes from her typewriter. She spends hours at the library researching (backseat traveling) new and interesting locations. Ms. Douglass lives with her husband and three sons in Massachusetts.

Dear Reader:

SILHOUETTE DESIRE is an exciting new line of contemporary romances from Silhouette Books. During the past year, many Silhouette readers have written in telling us what other types of stories they'd like to read from Silhouette, and we've kept these comments and suggestions in mind in developing SILHOUETTE DESIRE.

DESIREs feature all of the elements you like to see in a romance, plus a more sensual, provocative story. So if you want to experience all the excitement, passion and joy of falling in love, then SILHOUETTE DESIRE is for you.

I hope you enjoy this book and all the wonderful stories to come from SILHOUETTE DESIRE. I'd appreciate any thoughts you'd like to share with us on new SILHOUETTE DESIRE, and I invite you to write to us at the address below:

Karen Solem
Editor-in-Chief
Silhouette Books
P.O. Box 769
New York, N.Y. 10019

BILLIE DOUGLASS
Sweet Serenity

Silhouette Desire

Published by Silhouette Books New York

America's Publisher of Contemporary Romance

Other Silhouette Books by Billie Douglass

Search for a New Dawn
A Time to Love
Knightly Love

 SILHOUETTE BOOKS, a Simon & Schuster Division of
GULF & WESTERN CORPORATION
1230 Avenue of the Americas, New York, N.Y. 10020

Copyright © 1983 by Barbara Delinsky

Distributed by Pocket Books

ISBN: 0-671-45839-6

First Silhouette Books printing January, 1983

10 9 8 7 6 5 4 3 2 1

America's Publisher of Contemporary Romance

Printed in the U.S.A.

To sweet lovers of the world

Sweet Serenity

1

～≈≈≈≈≈≈≈≈≈≈～

Humming softly, Serena Strickland gave a final tug to the ribbon she'd just tied, cocked her head in appraisal of her work, then grinned. It was perfect! Mint chocolate peas and carrots in a clear canning jar ringed and crowned with a lavish orange polka dot bow—the effect was gay enough to make even the most skeptical Minneapolitan believe that spring was around the corner.

Shifting on the high stool behind the counter, she looked up past rows of goody-filled canisters to the front of the shop and beyond, where the sun splashed teasingly through the Crystal Court. Serena couldn't restrain a knowing smile as the crisp rays bounced from column to column, storefront to storefront in the plaza, darting in and around in a game of hide and seek all too appropriate, she thought, for this April Fool's Day.

It had been a long winter, true to Minnesota legend. The snow still lay in mounds at the far ends of parking lots and driveways or beneath trees against which it had drifted and whose shade now shielded it from the melting power of the sun. And, yes, she mused with a note of realism, it would probably snow again before the muck underfoot dried into memory. Five years' living in this most northern of the central states cautioned her against unqualified optimism. But spring would come; she felt it in her freckles. Scattered from cheek to cheek over the bridge of her nose, they were faded now, ready to pop into vivid life with the first of the springtime sun. In anticipation, she flipped the calendar to April 1.

The gentle jangle of the front door bell called her from her daydreams to the world at hand. Approaching without hesitation was a man she'd never seen before. He wore a three-piece suit, an open khaki trenchcoat, and a decidedly desperate expression.

"May I help you?" She stood quickly, but had no time to move from behind the counter before the man reached her. At closer range he seemed less sure of himself, almost embarrassed.

He took a deep breath. "Have you got something called . . . Pretzel Joys?" he finally blurted out. "My wife is expecting a baby any day now and says she's got to have some. She's a regular customer of yours."

"Joan! You must be Joan Miller's husband!" Serena's hazel eyes widened as she broke into an open smile of recognition, then grew suddenly apprehensive. "How *is* she? It's been awhile since I've seen her. I wondered whether she'd had the baby yet."

Jonathan Miller grimaced. "She's a week overdue and very uncomfortable. I only wish there was more that *I* could do. So if my picking up Pretzel Joys will make her happy, Pretzel Joys she'll have." He paused in a moment of doubt. "You *do* have them, don't you?"

"Of course!" Serena laughed, rounding the counter and reaching for a glass canister. "And if I didn't have them here, I'd have had some sent special delivery from the manufacturer in Chicago. How much would you like?"

The father-to-be frowned. "I don't know—a pound, maybe two. What would you recommend? *You* know Joan."

Nodding through her laughter, Serena began to weigh scoops of the individually wrapped candies into a brightly patterned bag that matched the walls of the store with its lime-green and fresh pink bamboo design. "I think that two pounds should hold her for a while. If she needs more she can call and I'll have them delivered." Out of habit, she handed a sample to her customer. "Would you like to try one?"

"Oh no," he laughed. "I've got enough bad habits without looking for any new ones." But he picked one up and scrutinized it closely. "What *are* they made of, anyway?"

Serena shoveled in the last of the two pounds, then went to the ribbon rack to tie a cheerful bow on the handle of the pint-sized shopping bag. "They're crushed pretzels rolled into a ball of creamy white chocolate. Do you mean to say that Joan's been hoarding them all this time?"

His low-grumbled "'Fraid so" was offered jokingly. "I never knew how much they meant to her until last night—uh, make that one o'clock this morning. I can assure you that she'll be pleased to see this bag!" After paying for his purchase he swept up the item and headed for the door.

"My best to Joan, and good luck to you both!" Serena called after him before turning to help a customer who had entered at his departure.

For an April Fool's Day the morning passed without shock. Customers came and went, many of them familiar faces stocking up on one or another of their favorite confections. Nancy Wadsworth, Serena's good friend and assistant, arrived at eleven to help sort through the deliveries in the back room while Serena held down the fort out front. With a pickup in activity during the noon hour, when workers from the office buildings surrounding the mall wandered in and out, both women worked side by side, dispensing and wrapping selections of imported suckers, novelty chocolates, and various and sundry jelly beans with the flair which had made the shop known throughout the sweet-circles of Minneapolis. By the time Serena grabbed her purse at one-thirty, she had earned her luncheon break.

"I'm off now, Nance," she stage-whispered to the other woman as the latter put a wide beribboned stopper on an oversized milk bottle filled with malted milk balls. "I'll be back in an hour or so."

"Say," Nancy asked her as the customer left, "did you see the new 'fun jars' that came in this morning? They're adorable—some have frogs on them, others have pigs or lady bugs. You'll have a grand time filling them!"

Serena beamed at the thought. The "interior decorating," as she liked to call the selection and arrangement of candies or nuts in each fancy container, was always a challenge. "Great! I'll take a look this afternoon. I've got to run now, though. I'm meeting André upstairs."

"André?" Nancy feigned a shiver. "Is this business or pleasure? There's something about him that makes me uneasy. Of all your men, I like *him* the least."

"*All my men?* Nancy, you make me sound positively wicked!"

"You're *not*, Serena. That's the trouble. You *should* let loose and have a fling *every* once in a while."

"Nancy!" Serena chided good-naturedly. "I'm surprised at you . . . a mother and all. . . ."

"My *daughter* happens to be twelve," her friend countered. "You're twenty-nine. There's a difference. You should even be thinking of settling down—"

"Nancy—"

"—but *not* with André. Perhaps with Ken or Rod or Gregory . . . but *not* with André."

Serena laughed. "I think you've made your point. Don't worry. André may come on a little strong, but he's really harmless." At Nancy's look of doubt, she added, "And he *is* my investment counselor. I've got to keep him on his toes."

"You can have him," her friend snorted softly, then raised her voice as Serena headed for the door, "but have a good lunch. He *owes* it to you!"

Throwing her head back in a half-laugh, Serena left the shop behind. Confident steps took her past neighboring windows, the broad panes of which reflected her slender form, a floating vision with a touch of sophistication. She wore a long-sleeved blouse of Burgundy silk, whose wide cuffs and collar were of a contrasting cream hue that matched the ivory of her lightly flared wool skirt. Her high-heeled pumps and the plush leather shoulder bag that hung by her hip matched the Burgundy of the blouse. If eyes turned at her passing she was too self-contained to notice. Within minutes André Phillips greeted her in the lobby of the restaurant, dashingly bestowing a kiss on each of her cheeks.

"And how's my favorite sweet lady today?" he exclaimed as he held her back to admire the heart-shaped face framed by thick auburn hair that swirled in waves to her shoulders.

"Sweet as ever," Serena quipped lightly. "And *you* must be having trouble readjusting to the U.S. of A."

"How could you tell?" With an arm thrown possessively over her shoulders, André led her to where the hostess stood awaiting his nod.

"*Both* cheeks, André?" Her gaze narrowed teasingly. "Very European." As the hostess beckoned for them to follow, Serena took advantage of the restaurant's closely set tables to pull from beneath his grasp and move out in front of him. Far from being blinded by his charm, she knew of the high style of life he treasured and, though it wasn't what she wanted, she indulged him in his excitement. Accepting the seat he held for her, she listened patiently as he recounted his Parisian adventures, and took each with a grain of salt.

It had been a month since she'd seen him. As he talked she watched him, acknowledging his good looks even as she stood by her conviction that his dark hair was a bit too neatly combed, his natty clothes a bit too carefully worn, his facial expressions a bit too deliberate for her total comfort. When she'd first sought investment advice several years ago the bank had recommended André as someone in the know. Indeed, his connections reached to the upper echelons of the Twin Cities' power elite. His life was, in his mind, at least, an exciting one.

Though she had dated him on occasion, Serena successfully kept him at arm's length. Thrice-married and thrice-divorced, André held no lure for her other than as the provider of a few entertaining hours of friendship and a large dose of investment advice. If the financial statements she received at regular intervals were to be believed, he had done well for her.

"So, tell me"—he broke off his dissertation to draw her into the conversation—"how goes *Sweet Serenity?*"

Serena pushed a thick lock of hair behind one ear. "The shop is doing just fine, André. I keep waiting for the slow spell that never seems to come. Not that I'm complaining, mind you. . . ." She smiled. "Here it is, the first of April. We've got Easter, May Day, Mother's Day, Memorial Day—you name it and it spells business."

André eyed her askance. "Do you mean to say that you have specials for April Fool's Day?"

"Sure." She was unfazed. "I sold several boxes of white chocolate golf balls this morning. They look like the real thing. Of course, they'll melt in the golfer's hand if he happens to hold onto one long enough. Then"—she grinned—"there are sets of toffee golf tees, tins of red licorice paper clips, bottles of marshmallow aspirin, hanging marzipan peperomia plants—"

14

"All right, all right! Sorry I asked!" He stemmed the onslaught with a chuckle. "But I'm glad to hear things are buzzing." Then, in the amount of time it took him to cut a piece of his pork chop, he sobered. Serena was always amazed at these sudden switches from lightness to intensity, but she'd long ago attributed them to nothing more than André's high-strung nature and quick mind. "Have you given any more thought to investing in the money fund we discussed before I left?"

Nibbling at her egg-and-avocado salad, Serena chose her words with care. "I've given it some thought, but . . . I'm also beginning to think along . . . other lines."

"Oh?"

"Uh-huh." With a deep breath she broached the topic she'd been toying with for months. "I'm considering opening a branch of *Sweet Serenity* in one of the suburban areas."

An odd silence preceded his "Oh?" No longer eating, he gave her his undivided attention. Serena met it in earnest.

"Downtown Minneapolis has been a fantastic market. But many of my clients come from the same areas that have made the large gourmet markets, Devlin's, for example, such a phenomenal success. People flock there from all over. It has an elegance, a sense of quality about it, that the population is both literally and figuratively eating up." She snickered at the pun, but felt a pang of discomfort when André obviously missed her humor. "You think it's a bad idea?"

He hesitated. "Don't you think it may be a little premature?"

Serena bit at her full lower lip before answering. She respected André's opinions and it bothered her that, even speaking as a friend, he wasn't as enthusiastic as she about the prospect of expansion. *"Sweet Serenity* has been a viable concern now for five years." She repeated the reasoning that had worked so well on herself. "I've been able to reinvest profits—you've done that for me—and we should have *no* trouble setting up a second shop."

"In Devlin's?"

"That would be nice," she drawled with a chuckle, "but I doubt we'd get the space in Saint Louis Park. Perhaps in one of the newer stores. Actually, I was hoping to find a spot in Edina or Wayzata."

André pursed his lips as he studied his plate. "I don't know, Serena. I think you should give it more thought." He shook his head, though not a hair budged from its designated spot. "With the instability of the economy and all . . ."

"Oh, it's still at the thinking stage," she was quick to reassure him, "but I wanted to explain why I'm skeptical about investing heavily in anything that might tie up my money for a long period. If I do decide to go ahead with this I may need to get my hands on some of my funds."

As quickly as he had sobered, André smiled. "You may put me out of business, you know."

And Serena then understood part of his hesitancy. After all, he earned his living making investments for businesspeople such as herself. Investments took capital; the more capital she sank into a new shop, the less there would be left to invest. "André," she chided, "would I do that to you? If I open a second store and it's even half as successful as the first I'll have twice as much money for you to play with. And, besides, my interests must be *peanuts* compared to most of your clients!"

He reached down and brought her hand to his lips, kissing its back in chivalrous fashion. "Very *tasty* peanuts, Serena. But . . . enough of business." He brightened. "Listen, I'm going out to L.A. next month. Why don't you join me?"

"Join you? André, I have a shop to run! I can't just take off and jet around the country!"

16

He quirked a brow. "Would you, if it weren't for the shop?"

It was actually a very simple question. For one thing, she had spent her early childhood in southern California. It had been the scene of her father's financial and emotional ruin. She had only painful memories of the area. For another, she had not been, nor ever would be, André's lover. And *that* was the crux of his present proposition.

When she spoke it was quietly and with just enough of an apology in her tone to offset the finality of her words. "No, André. You know that I wouldn't."

"Then I'm destined to bang my head against a brick wall?"

Serena deftly turned the tables on his teasing. "You've been through three awful marriages! You don't need another woman hanging on to you!"

But he was quick on the rebound. "Come on, Serena. When was the last time *you* ever hung on a man?" Her sheepish shrug spoke of her independence. "And you're not about to try it with me, are you?"

She shook her head slowly, her pout one of affection but far from anything more. "No. I'm afraid it's not in the cards for us." As the waiter appeared with their coffee a movement near André caught her eye. At the adjacent table a couple was in the process of being seated. The woman's back was to Serena. The man stood graciously by to hold her chair, then took the seat opposite, offering Serena a clear view of his face.

It held her instantly as a galvanic force ripped through her subconscious. She knew that face! Beyond a doubt, she knew that face! Yet she couldn't place it.

Details were lost in the overall image, whose familiarity rippled through her in repeating waves that stirred her pulse. This was no visage from recent experience. Instinct told her that. Rather, his face whisked her back over time as she sought a memory that was stubbornly elusive.

With a taut swallow she dragged her gaze away. Grasping at the nearest diversion, her coffee, she nearly scalded her mouth as she drank it too quickly.

André talked on. She smiled and nodded, participating only distractedly in his chatter. But the puzzle remained. Her attention was drawn back time and again to the man at the next table. She was so certain she'd seen him before. . . .

"What do you think, Serena?" André's question caught her off guard.

"Hmmm? I'm sorry." She shook her head clear of cobwebs. "I was hung up on something else. What were you saying?"

His patience was commendable. "I wondered," he stated slowly, "what you thought of the prospect of Minneapolis replacing Washington as the nation's capital."

"What?" Her laugh had a definite edge to it that had nothing to do with André's thought. "Are you serious?"

"I certainly am," he deadpanned. "There's been a rumor to that effect, you know."

"I didn't!"

"It's true. It's even been put into print that by the end of the century we may house the government workings out here."

The concept was preposterous enough to drive that nameless face from her mind and spark Serena to life. "Heaven forbid! Minneapolis is just fine the way it is. The last thing we need is an invasion from Washington—or any other area!"

"And how long did you say you'd been living here?" he teased. "You sound like a die-hard Minnesotan."

"Almost." She grinned, then lapsed into relative silence as her counselor delved into the business prospects of a governmental move, delighted with the fantasy. Serena interjected the appropriate uh-huhs and reallys, but again her mind had begun to wander.

18

She glanced once more at the next table. The man was engrossed in discussion with his companion, though he was listening more than speaking. With the first shock yielding to frustration, Serena studied his features in search of a clue.

His hair was dark brown, rich and full, the sprinkles of gray in his well-tapered sideburns putting him around the forty-year mark. His nose was straight, his lips firm, his eyes hazel, like her own. He wore a shirt and tie, blazer and slacks, presenting a dignified though sporty appearance that was far from riveting but totally masculine. That he was attractive was unquestionable, and, at the moment, irrelevant. There was something beyond his outward appearance that nagged at her. She stared helplessly at him as the spark of familiarity shot through her again. It settled in her gut in an inexplicable response that shook her complacency and rattled her self-confidence. *Who was he?*

As though in response to her silent plea he looked up. In a moment of inner cataclysm for Serena he caught her eye. *She* caught her breath. As placid as he appeared on the surface, the force of his gaze spoke of a deep inner fire. That was what seemed most familiar to her. Mouth dry, she stared, unable to look away as long as his gaze held hers. His expression held a question, perhaps even faint amusement. Strangely, though, he mirrored none of the recognition she so strongly felt. Could she be mistaken? . . .

When he finally returned his attention to his companion Serena felt drained. Facing André once more, she was too preoccupied to miss his fleeting uncertainty, but he talked on and quickly forgot her diversion. Slowly she finished her coffee. Once more she looked toward the next table; once more her gaze was met. André recaptured her attention with a witty review of the improvisational theater troupe he had seen the night before in Cedar-Riverside. But he lost her a final time to the nameless memory whose eyes shone brightly toward hers.

For Serena it was a disconcerting experience. She'd always been good with names and faces. It was necessary in her business, a small touch that her customers appreciated. But here was someone whose identity mystified her. Moreover, something kept her from alerting André to the man's presence, though he knew almost every distinguished face in the Minneapolis–Saint Paul area.

And this face *was,* in its unpretentious way, distinguished, even aside from the quiet ring of authority in his gaze. Serena devoted a few final moments, as André studied the bill, to solving her mystery. Much as she tried, she could pin neither a name nor a place to this man whose interest was now mercifully centered on his woman-friend, granting Serena as free a perusal as convention would allow.

Then, quite unwittingly, he threw another wrench in the works by smiling. It was devastating in its intensity and totally unique. Had she ever seen that smile before Serena would have recalled it. No, she hadn't seen *it,* but she had seen *him,* of that she was certain.

"I'd watch out for him, Serena." André's warning was soft and spoken with a note of earnestness that stunned her.

"Wh–what?" Had she been that obvious?

"That man behind me—"

"You know him?" she interrupted on impulse.

"No. He must be new, perhaps passing through."

She frowned. "Then why the warning?"

André rose smoothly and came to stand behind her. Bending low in a proprietary attitude, one hand on either of her shoulders, he put his mouth close by her ear. Though Serena couldn't get herself to look up, she sensed his eyes on the next table.

"I have feelings about people. That one strikes me as an agitator."

"An agitator?" she murmured out of the corner of her mouth. "He looks harmless enough to me."

"Is that why you've been staring?"

She couldn't move without André's say-so; she was cornered in every sense. "He . . . looks familiar. That's all. I'm sure I've seen him somewhere, but I can't place him."

André straightened, deftly pulling out her chair and drawing her up in one fluid move. "A mystery man from your lurid past?" he teased her lightly, but she cringed as she draped the strap of her bag over her shoulder, opting for sarcasm as a cover.

"No doubt." Her drawl wafted into the air as the hand at her back guided her from the restaurant. She hadn't had to look at the man again to have his face imprinted in her mind.

There it stayed, in living color, to torment her through the afternoon. Each idle moment brought forth the vision with renewed force. *Where had she seen him?*

Running *Sweet Serenity* provided some respite, deflecting her attention to her customers. However, with the help of Nancy, who left to fetch her teenagers at three, and Monica, a teenager who arrived soon after from school, much of Serena's time was free for "decorating." Her hands were kept busy, carrying out the directives of her mind, while the latter was free to wander.

Inch by inch and working backward from the present, she scoured the years in an attempt to locate that empty slot crying out to be filled. Her past five years had been spent here in Minneapolis, building *Sweet Serenity* from scratch with the money she had unexpectedly inherited from her maternal grandfather. Even now, as she looked around the shop with pride, she recalled the surprise with which she'd received the bequest. Following her father's disgrace, her mother's family had been less than supportive. The fact that a grandfather she'd barely known had entrusted her with such a substantial sum after her father had squandered both dollars and trust had been an added incentive for making a success of the shop.

Five years in Minneapolis. The occasional trip to Seattle to visit her mother and younger brother, Steve, with whom the older, sadly defeated woman lived. Periodic trips to Chicago to attend gift shows or negotiate directly with her suppliers. Had there been, during this time, any man such as the one whose presence had struck such a jarring inner chord today? To her knowledge—no.

Traveling further back, she reviewed the two years she'd spent in Boston managing the Quincy Market boutique that had been the original inspiration for *Sweet Serenity*. During this period she had found herself, gaining self-confidence as a creative and capable woman, self-supporting for the first time and slowly beginning to rebuild her dreams. They were dreams different from those of the naive young girl she had been so long ago, but they were lovely in their own way.

Two years in Boston. Customers coming and going. The occasional date for dinner, a concert, or a show. Many familiar faces, mostly friendly. A landlord, several interesting tenants. A doctor, a dentist, and, of course, the members of the racquetball club. Were there any faces among the lot that resembled this April Fool's Day apparition? No.

The four years she had spent in North Carolina as an undergraduate student at Duke were even harder to examine in detail. Not only was the time more distant, but she had been thrown into the passing company of many, many more people. Students, teachers, house mothers, administrators. Closing her eyes tightly against the peace of *Sweet Serenity* she envisioned her college life, scanning the crowd of faces in her memory for the one whose hidden fire had seared her consciousness today. Nothing. The age was wrong. The face was wrong. Nothing!

In an uncharacteristic fit of frustration Serena crushed the bow she'd been attempting to shape for a crystal martini shaker filled with liquor-stuffed mint olives. *Who was he?*

Intuitively she knew his was no face seen merely in passing at some random point in her life. His gaze had affected her too deeply for that. He had been *someone*—someone important. In retrospect she felt a strange defensiveness, a need to protect herself—though from what she simply didn't know. Perhaps she had to go further back. But each year's regression was more painful.

Seeking escape, she tossed the ruined ribbon into the wastebasket, left the countertop at which she'd been working and rescued Monica from the clutches of long-winded Mrs. McDermott, a regular fan of cognac cordials. After Mrs. McDermott came several clusters of adolescents intent on splurging on one of the exotic flavors of jelly beans or—the current rage among them—gummy bears. Personally, Serena couldn't stand the things. For that matter, she rarely ate any of her wares, sampling them only for the purpose of describing them to customers. Mrs. McDermott, for instance, a sprightly senior citizen, would not have been terribly pleased when the gummy bears stuck to teeth that Serena suspected were removable. On the other hand, it was the mature patrons who could appreciate the rich milk chocolate of the imported candies as youngsters could not. So much of Serena's service involved learning and respecting the tastes of her clientele. It was for this reason that so many had become habitual indulgers since she'd opened her doors.

"Mrs. French!" She burst into a smile as a favorite customer entered the shop. "How are you?"

"Just fine, Serena," the attractive woman replied. "But I need your help."

"What's the problem?" Over the years June French had had "problems" ranging from office parties to Little League banquets to numerous get-well gifts and other more conventional items.

"How about a sweet sixteen sleepover? I need party favors for seven teenaged girls, *all* of them fighting acne, baby fat, and eleven o'clock curfews!"

"I remember too well," Serena quipped. In truth she had never been to a sleepover, much less a sweet sixteen party. At that particular point in her life she had been a loner. But acne, baby fat, and curfews—those she could relate to. "Let me think. . . ."

Slowly she looked around the shop. Along the left-hand wall ran the stacks of oversized canisters whose transparent glass faces displayed goods on sale by the pound. Along the right were shelves of decorative boxes and containers, a sampling of which were filled and wrapped for instant sale.

Tapping a tapered forefinger against her lips, she deliberated. "Of course! The obvious." Several short strides brought her to a shelf that held small, hand-painted tins. Kneeling on the low-pile green carpet, she gathered a selection of tins together. Then she turned to the opposite wall. "Lo-cal suckers. They're fun. Here"— she plucked one of the wrapped candies from its canister and offered it to her customer—"try this. It's tangerine. There are also licorice, raspberry, butterscotch, lime and rum. We can fill each tin with a mixed sampling and tie a different colored bow around each. When the candy is gone the tin can be used for earrings, pins, you name it."

The nod that accompanied Mrs. French's grin vouched for her delight. "You've done it again, Serena. I only wish all my problems were so easily solved."

So did Serena . . . with respect to her own. For as the hours passed and memory persisted in failing her she grew more agitated.

Returning to work behind the counter, she let her mind drift further back to those years she'd spent with her aunt and uncle in New York. Those had been her high school years, right after her father's fall from grace. There had been anonymity in New York, something she had craved after the harrowing experience of stigmatization left her bruised and sensitive. She had spent those years quietly, her peers indifferent to her past. Only one, Michael Lowry, had used it against her, and the memory still hurt.

To hell with this strange man's identity. It wasn't worth the effort of rehashing those years. If she was ever to learn his name it would be destiny that chose the time and place. She'd done everything she could to ferret it out from the annals of her memory, with no success whatsoever. Enough! She had *Sweet Serenity,* today and tomorrow. The past was done!

Buoyed by her newfound determination, she lent Monica a hand with the steady flow of customers during the predictably busy late afternoon hours. Then, when the rush had finally eased, she started packaging the telephone orders they had received in the course of the day. There were several orders to be sent to area hospitals, several to be delivered to private homes. These would be handled with care by the local delivery service she retained. There were also several orders to be shipped long distance. Each required careful and extensive padding with the bright lime tissue she always used when wrapping or cushioning sales. In those cases where more glass than usual was involved she dug into the stack of newspapers in the back room to supplement the gayer tissue as padding.

Standing behind the counter, she could absently supervise the activity in the shop as she worked. Nonchalantly she reached toward the newspaper, which she crumpled loosely and eased into one of the boxes before her. Three, four, five times she repeated the process until the package was closed, sealed, and its shipping label affixed. Then she began on the next box. She reached for a piece of newspaper, crumpled it—

Reynolds. The name leapt up from the half-crumpled newsprint, slamming her with the force of a truck, freezing her hand in midair, halting the flow of air in her lungs as her heart beat furiously. *Reynolds.* With unsteady fingers she straightened the paper, pressing the creases out with her palms, nervously spreading the sheet atop the counter. The name had been there, buried deep in the recesses of her mind. It took a minute of searching for her to locate the article and she was filled with trepidation as she read it.

MINNEAPOLIS, March 20. The *Tribune* has learned that its major competitor, the *Twin City Bulletin,* has been bought by Thomas Harrison Reynolds of the Harrison Publishing Group. Originally from Los Angeles, Mr. Reynolds takes the helm after months of negotiations, during which he bid heavily against two eastern corporations for ownership of the *Bulletin* and its subsidiary press. Initial reports filtering from *Bulletin* executive offices indicate that the staff will temporarily remain intact as Mr. Reynolds studies its effectiveness. The new publisher has vowed to improve the quality of reporting and . . .

Reynolds. Thomas Harrison Reynolds. A name for the face. And a place. Los Angeles. A time. Sixteen years ago. Tom Reynolds, the cub reporter who had first broken the story that eventually led to her father's indictment on charges of embezzlement.

It had to be a hoax. Serena reread the small article and moaned. Knees weak, she slouched against a high stool for support. Why here? *Why here?* Minneapolis was *her* home now. Here there was nothing to haunt her. She had a happy present and an optimistic future. Of all the places into which Tom Reynolds might have dug his journalistic claws, *why here?*

Tom Reynolds. It certainly explained the gut response she'd had earlier. Even now his name stormed through her, leaving tension in its wake. The last time she had seen him had been in court. Thirteen at the time, she had been vulnerable and impressionable. And Tom Reynolds had impressed her as being hard, ambitious, and . . . wrong.

As she struggled to assimilate the fact of his presence in Minneapolis, her eye fell on the calendar she'd changed just this morning. April 1. April Fool's Day. Was this all an ugly gag?

In her heart she knew it wasn't, even before she looked toward the front of the shop when she heard the bell. There at her door stood none other than the man in question, Thomas Harrison Reynolds.

2

~~~~~~~~~~~~~~~

For a fleeting moment Serena was back in that Los Angeles County courtroom, with Thomas Harrison Reynolds standing boldly among the throng of press personnel covering the trial. He had been sixteen years younger then and his appearance had reflected it, from the shaggy fall of hair across his brow to the faded corduroys and worn loafers above which a blazer, patched at the elbows, seemed a begrudging concession to courtroom convention.

Now the corduroys had been replaced by gray wool slacks, the loafers by polished cordovans. Today's blazer was navy, immaculately cut, well-fitted. Sixteen years had handsomely matured his skin and dashed the silver wisps she'd noticed earlier through his hair. But his eyes and the depth of his expression hadn't changed a bit. On their power she was hauled forward over the years.

Tom stood at the door, Serena behind the waist-high counter. Twenty feet separated them, twenty feet charged with waves of electricity. Caught in the middle was Monica, looking from one face to the other, instantly sensing something unusual astir.

Serena would never know why the shop had suddenly grown quiet. Where had the customers who had been milling around moments before disappeared to?

As though to further the developing nightmare Monica, seventeen and infinitely perceptive, slipped softly past her. "I'll unload those late deliveries, Serena," she said, then was gone.

For the first time in recent memory Serena didn't know what to do. One part of her felt like that frightened thirteen-year-old back in Los Angeles; the other part was a poised and successful twenty-nine-year-old business-woman. Somewhere in the middle of the two she waffled. Why was he here? What did he want now?

Paralysis seized her; she was helpless to function. In the span of what seemed hours, yet could have been no more than a minute or two, she felt raked over the coals for a crime in which she'd had no part. Tom's gaze grilled her with the persistence of an inquisitor. Beneath its force the knot in her stomach spread slowly through her system.

Then, as though in partial answer to the prayer she hadn't had the presence to offer, the door opened and another customer entered the shop. Tom moved easily to the side, stopping to lean casually against the wall by the door.

A flicker of annoyance passed through Serena that he should post himself so confidently on her terrain. The thought was enough to stiffen her backbone. If it was a demonstration he wanted, a demonstration he'd get. This *was* her turf. Satisfying customers *was* her specialty. That Thomas Reynolds should presume to intimidate her in her own shop galled her.

Only he could see the fire in her eyes as she left the safe haven of her counter to approach the newcomer. In her determination to ignore him Serena missed the hint of a smile that both curved his lips slightly and sparkled in his eyes.

As much in defiance as in deference to the customer, she put a purposeful smile on her face. "May I help you?" she asked the middle-aged woman who, from the moment she'd entered the shop, had been entranced so by the cheery array of goodies around her that Serena's approach startled her.

"Oh! Uh, yes!" She looked up quickly, then was drawn helplessly back to a dainty, hand-sewn pocketbook, child-sized and filled with individually wrapped suckers. "This is adorable. I want to pick up something for my granddaughter. This might be just the thing. Today's her birthday."

"How old is she?" Serena asked, noting out of the corner of her eye that Tom had straightened and begun to look around the shop himself.

The older woman grinned. "Just seven, God bless her!"

Tom moved slowly in their direction, idling nonchalantly before various items, but moving onward nonetheless. Serena grasped at the escape hatch opened by her customer. "Seven. How wonderful! May I make a suggestion?"

"By all means."

"I could fill *that* bag," she pointed to the small pocketbook that had charmed the woman, "with Jelly Bean Hash." Without waiting for approval she retreated toward the rear of the shop, as far as possible from where Tom had paused to pick up and study an oriental lacquered box, to the crystal cookie jar set prominently on a corner of her work-counter. It was filled to the brim with Jelly Bean Hash.

"Jelly Bean Hash?" the woman echoed Serena, her question echoed in its turn by Tom's dark brows, which rose as he looked Serena's way in wry amusement.

30

Serena concentrated on the sale. Lifting the lid of the cookie jar, she removed one of the cookie-shaped candies with the scoop left nearby for the purpose. "Assorted jelly beans dropped into a white chocolate 'batter.' Kids adore them. The purse will hold perhaps half a dozen. I could wrap them in colored plastic wrap to match the fabric of the bag, if you like."

Beaming, the woman nodded. "I would like that. Thank you. It sounds perfect."

To Serena's temporary relief Tom had gone back to his studies. She set to work wrapping the hash in deep red plastic to match the bag her customer had chosen, then tied a vibrant yellow bow around the whole. "There!" She held up the finished product for inspection before sinking it in a bag. "How's that?"

As the woman expressed her pleasure and paid for her purchase Tom silently nodded his approval, too. Even this peripheral participation in the exchange rattled Serena, who seemed to spend longer fumbling for the correct change of the twenty-dollar bill the woman offered than she'd spent recommending and wrapping the item.

With each step the woman took toward the front door Tom moved closer to Serena, who grew increasingly uneasy. She had never felt so awkward. Could she treat this man as simply another customer? Could she pretend, after the intensity of their exchanged glances that she had never seen him before?

The shop was quiet, with only the intermittent rustle of Monica working in the back room to break the silence. Despite the absurdity of the situation Serena couldn't quite find any words with which to break the ice. As she lifted her eyes from her clenched hands, her own fear and resentment clashed in silent battle with the curiosity and confusion in his gaze. *Why didn't he say something? What was he up to?* If only Monica were out here with her

31

to serve as a buffer. But that was the cowardly approach, she chided herself. Then, once more, she was saved by the bell.

"Serena!" A tall bundle of knee-length rabbit fur and shimmering red-gold tresses surged through the front door, crossing the room before the jangle of the bell had died. "I need Red Hots! You've got some, haven't you? Oh, excuse me—" Cynthia Wayne came to an abrupt stop beside Tom, her striking blue eyes wide. "I can wait, if you're busy." Her gaze didn't budge.

"No, no, that's fine," said Serena, enthusiastically recovering the use of her tongue. "It's good to see you, Cynthia." *She would never know how good!* For the first time in the four years that she and Cynthia had been weekly racquetball partners Serena actually welcomed Cynthia's very blatant sensuality. Anything to sidetrack Thomas Harrison Reynolds from his enigmatic quest. "You sound desperate," she teased her friend. "Any problem?"

Cynthia faced her and grinned mischievously. "Nothing a pound of your spicy little Cinnamon Red Hots can't solve." Narrowing her gaze at the assortment of Chinese-style takeout containers on a shelf behind the counter, she pointed to one. "I think that blue-and-white-checked job over there should blend just beautifully with his office."

Though Serena was uncomfortably aware of Tom following the conversation closely, she couldn't resist a soft-spoken jab at her friend's humor. "Now, now, Cynthia. Who is it you're trying to burn?" Behind Cynthia, Tom smirked.

"My boss, as it happens." She tilted her chin up in revolt. "He's been really short with all of us today. I'd like to see him take a handful of these and stuff them in his mouth with his usual greed. *Then* he'll have something to bark at!"

"He'll be breathing fire," Serena warned her lightly.

"He deserves it," the other woman shot back. Full lips curved into a seductive pout, Cynthia tossed a sidelong glance at Tom. His eyes, however, were firmly trained on Serena.

If Monica had been perceptive beyond her years, Cynthia's insight was a product of hers. Had she not been in a rush to get back to the office she might have been tempted to stay and chat with her friend. Had this man, whom Serena had notably failed to introduce to her, not been standing by waiting patiently for an unknown something from Serena, Cynthia would have lingered even in spite of her boss's decree. She was a born flirt; but she also knew when a man was irrevocably indifferent to her charm. And this man *was*. Her provocative appearance hadn't sparked him in the least. With a sigh she took her purchase from Serena's outstretched hand.

"Thanks, love," she murmured in answer to her friend's feeble excuse for a smile. Both women walked to the front door.

"Go easy on him, Cyn," Serena quipped when she knew they were out of Tom's earshot. She was unprepared for her friend's retort.

"On him? What about you?" Her whisper stopped as she glanced back over her shoulder at Tom. "What's going on with *him?*"

"Nothing."

"He's gorgeous."

"I really hadn't noticed." They stood now at the opened door, Serena with her back purposefully to the inside of the shop.

"Come on, Serena. I know you're not a wild dater, but he's not here for gum drops." In the face of Serena's helpless expression, Cynthia knew she would get no information beyond what she had observed herself. There was definitely something going on between her friend and the dark-haired man in her shop. Perhaps Serena would tell her more when they played. "I'll see you at the club tomorrow night, love."

"Sure, Cyn."

"Take care!"

Despite the unmistakably naughty drawl in the red-head's voice, Serena watched her departure with reluctance. The furred form flew on down the stairs toward the street level of the plaza, then disappeared through a doorway to the outside world.

Serena sighed. Then, with a deep breath and a longer sigh, she turned.

The soft carpet had silenced Tom's footsteps as he had approached. A gasp of fright escaped her when she found herself face to face with him. Face to face? It was more a case of face to throat! Standing at such close proximity with no buffer between them, Serena was appalled at the discrepancy in their height. The intensity of his expression, laced heavily now with amusement at her discomfort, was intimidating enough without this added leverage he seemed suddenly to have gained.

Lips dry, she bit her tongue to keep from wetting them in a gesture she knew would be misleading. Her heart beat double-time; her legs were momentarily shaky. Clearing her throat, she took a breath to begin—then stopped. Something . . . something in his expression brought back to mind the bizarre thought that had raced quickly through it earlier in the restaurant. Was there a possibility that he had *not* recognized her? Could some other unfathomable purpose have brought him into *Sweet Serenity?* For an instant she was aghast at the realization of how rude she had been, if that was the case. Then she reminded herself that it was Thomas Harrison Reynolds who stood before her. Straightening, she steeled herself to confront the enemy.

For lack of a better opening she slipped into the role of

shopkeeper. "May I help you?" Her tone was as even as she could produce under the circumstances, but it was far from completely self-confident. Chin up, body taut, she was mindful of the thudding in her chest.

Tom drew his brows together, then frowned more deeply. As he peered down his face held a mixture of varied and fleeting emotions. Many were the same she had sensed in him earlier—confusion, curiosity, skepticism, boldness, determination. There was still that noticeable absence of recognition—but there was also the presence of that fire, burning through the flickering hazel of his gaze. And there was something else deep within . . . working its way to the surface. . . .

To Serena's consternation, he put his head back and laughed. Only after he caught his breath did she hear his voice for the first time in sixteen years. It was smooth and steady, not as deep or gruff as she would have imagined, and it carried a gentleness totally at odds with her expectations.

"You *are* a character!" he marveled, confounding her further.

"Wh–what?"

"You're very unusual."

"Oh?"

"Uh-huh."

She paused. Would he declare his purpose? "Well . . . ?"

"Well, what?"

"Is there something I can do for you?" Her voice had risen in pitch along with her body heat.

"I hope so," he drawled, butter smooth. This was not at all what she had expected.

"Are you looking for something?"

"Could be."

The conversation was going nowhere. Only her heart tripped recklessly forward, sending blood through her

veins at breakneck speed. She sighed. "You're staring."
Where was Monica?

"So are you," he rejoined, undaunted.

So she had been, though not of her own volition. It
was as though that fire in his eyes drew her; she had no
choice. Mustering the fragments of her self-possession,
she tore her gaze from his and walked quickly behind the
counter to finish the packing that had been so abruptly
interrupted by her discovery of this man's identity.

In a move she might later question she thrust the single
condemning sheet of newsprint to the side for safekeeping and completed the chore. Though her fingers
fumbled busily, her mind couldn't escape the absurdity of
the situation. Did he recognize her or not? In either case,
what did he want?

"Are you buying a gift for someone?" She tried again,
looking at him over the counter. He had come to stand
flush against it, his forearm resting on its raised rim. His
hand was long, strong, relaxed, clean—much as its
owner who, for the first time, seemed to grow impatient.

"Of course not. I'm here to see *you.*"

"About what?" she came back too quickly, apprehensive once more.

Her fear puzzled him nearly as much as his motive
alarmed her. Before either of them could say another
word the jangle of the bell offered a respite. With a
meaningful nod in the direction of the oncoming customer Tom stood to the side as Serena moved forward. Five
minutes later, having sold one wire chick filled with
oversized coconut jelly beans, she was back at ringside.
Tom picked up where they had left off.

"What about? I was hoping *you* could tell me that. It's
not every day that a woman in a restaurant eyes me the
way you did today."

"Oh?" What else could she say without tipping her
hand. If he truly didn't remember her *she* had the upper
hand. While one half of her ached to cry out its bitterness

toward him, the other half exerted good sense and stifled the words.

"I still can't figure it out." He continued to scrutinize her closely.

"What?"

"Those very pointed daggers you threw at me during lunch."

Had she been more obvious than she'd thought? Or had she simply been unaware of the strength of her mysterious resentment? "Daggers? I . . . you . . . you just looked . . . familiar. . . ."

"Hmm." He offered a crooked smile that lacked any humor. "You must have some enemy!"

How right he was, she mused sadly. If only he'd never moved to Minneapolis! If only she'd never had cause to remember him and the past he had helped to warp!

"How did you find me?" she asked softly.

Tom was pleased by her curiosity, a definite improvement on curtness. The warmth of his gaze was suddenly contagious, spreading over his features, threatening to extend to her own. She fought it by looking away.

"After you left I asked the hostess about you. She suggested I try *Sweet Serenity.* She also said"—there was humor in his tone—"that I'd have to wait in line."

Serena laughed innocently. "That might be true just before Christmas, Valentine's Day or Mother's Day. But, as you can see, on normal days we keep things moving."

"I don't think that was quite what she meant." One dark brow arched chidingly.

"Oh?" It took her a minute to catch on.

"Will you have dinner with me tonight?"

His invitation was so guileless that it made the situation that much worse. *"What?* How can you even suggest such a thing?"

He shrugged. "It's really not so unusual. Men and women do it all the time. I seem to recall that you had a very attentive luncheon partner."

"So did you," she lashed back, then blushed.

"Ah, you noticed. You *see*," he grinned playfully, "it *is* fairly common. How about it?"

Serena shook her head in amazement. How had she found herself in this situation? "This is ridiculous," she whispered, half to herself.

But he was fast to call her on it. "How so?"

Slowly she tipped her head back to face him. He was very attractive and, in all probability, very interesting. Had things been different she might have been tempted. As things stood, however, it was out of the question. She could never betray her father's memory by socializing with Tom Reynolds.

"You don't even know me," she hedged.

"That can be remedied," he countered.

"I could be married."

"To your lunch date?"

"He's my investment counselor."

"Ahh," he sighed softly. "But you did go to lunch with him. Why not dinner with me?"

"I had a good reason to have lunch with André. I don't have *any* reason to have dinner with you."

When he grinned the echo of his smile tingled strangely through her. "You just might enjoy yourself."

"I just might *not!*"

He frowned, perplexed. "Do you have a reason *not* to have dinner with me?"

"Yes."

"You *are* attached?"

"No. . . ."

"Then why not dinner?" he persisted.

Serena enjoyed a momentary feeling of power. "You look surprised, Mr. Reynolds. What's wrong—not used to being turned down?"

Tom grew alert. Straightening his shoulders, he took control once more. "You *know* me." His gaze narrowed with the flat statement. "I had that impression. How is that?"

"I . . . I read about you in the newspaper."

Her stammer fell victim to his slow headshake. "No good. The papers carried no photographs. I've been insistent about that."

"Insistent?" She was temporarily sidetracked by curiosity.

"Anonymity is something I prize," he stated simply.

"Hah! This must be a recent twist!" she scoffed in spontaneous sarcasm. Sixteen years ago Tom Reynolds had come brashly forward to denounce her father, first in print, then in court. She could almost hear the bang of the judge's gavel, then she realized it was the birth of a headache.

Every bit the investigator, Tom prodded further, which did nothing to discourage her headache. "You didn't learn my identity from the paper, Serena," he called her by name. *Thank you, Cynthia*, she mused wryly, then trembled. It was only a matter of time before he knew the truth. "You've known me in the past. Why don't I know you?" His features formed a deeper frown.

Her patience began to wane. "Could be that you've known so many women in your life you can't keep them straight. A dime a dozen?" She had sputtered at him in pure anger, heedless that her words were inappropriate. She was quickly sorry.

Retribution took the form not of anger but of smooth seduction. Tom's gaze fell from her eyes to the soft and vulnerable curve of her lips, lingering long enough to send a new and unwelcome tremor through her. "I've never dated you," he said huskily as his eyes made a slow exploration of her pale cheeks, the lazy auburn curls that fell there, the path of faded freckles across her nose. "I'd certainly remember you if I had. You're different. . . ."

Once more Serena was stunned into momentary sympathy by the innocence that surmounted even seduction. His inner struggle was obvious as he tried in vain to place her, much as she had wrestled with her own memory for the bulk of the afternoon. After all, she scowled grudgingly, what cause would he have to remember each of the stories he had covered, the subjects he had made or broken with the casual power of his pen? What cause would he have to consider the hapless families which his journalistic fervor had destroyed? Different, he had called her.

"I should hope so," she said with fiery indignation.

"Then, where . . . ?" His head jerked toward the door in irritation when the front bell rang again. Lips thinned into a grimace, he stepped aside more reluctantly now.

Serena, however, was grateful for the interruption. With an outward calm belying both the jitters in her stomach and the ache behind her forehead she dished up a pound-and-a-half order of Ice Cordials, wrapped them, bagged them, received payment for them—all the while drawing out each step as though she were headed for the gallows when she was through. By the time her customer left the ache had developed into a dull throb and she felt as pale and iced as the candies she'd just sold. Distressed, she cast a glance toward Tom, whose impatience was obvious, but under control.

"As I was asking"—he straightened and stalked her—"before we were so rudely interrupt—"

"*Serena?*" Monica's loud call from the back room, followed by her r ʻfled appearance, was as reassuring to Serena as it was irksome to Tom. The fire in his gaze seemed ready to escape its confines; Serena escaped first.

"Yes, Monica?" She turned to her young employee.

"I'm sorry to bother you." Monica looked timidly toward Tom, then lowered her voice for Serena's ears,

40

"but I've got a problem with the new shipment of trail mix. It looks weird." She crinkled her nose. "There's pink stuff sprinkled in it!"

"Here, let me see." Without a word to Tom, Serena disappeared into the back room. She recognized the problem instantly and returned to the front of the store to phone the distributor and report a spill of strawberry confetti chips.

"All set?" Tom asked when she finally replaced the receiver on its cradle. Like an old friend, he leaned casually against the counter.

"Yes. We'll get a new shipment tomorrow."

"What is this . . . trail mix, anyway?"

She smiled wanly. "It's a mixture of nuts and dried fruits—cashews, walnuts, raisins, dried apricots, pine-apple, banana. We sell a lot of it for—"

"—the trail?" The glint of humor in his eyes brought a helpless grin to her lips.

"For the trail. I only hope we won't have many trail-goers in for it between now and tomorrow after-noon."

"Does this kind of thing happen often?"

Serena grimaced. "Not very, thank goodness. I mean, there are always small problems here and there,"—she rubbed her temple absently—"but it's unusual when an entire shipment is bad." Her head shot up. "This isn't an investigation, is it? Are you looking for corruption in the candy business?" What had started as a quip developed into an indictment. "You aren't hoping to find someone worthy of assassination *here*, are you?"

His eyes flared, but he remained calm. "No, Serena. I don't do investigative reporting any more. And even if I did, this would be an unlikely spot for me to start searching."

"You'd be surprised." Her eyes narrowed angrily. "It's the most unlikely spots that often get hit!" Her thoughts

41

were of her father, who had always been an upstanding member of the community. Why had Tom gone after him?

Tom sensed her anguish. "Look, is there somewhere we can talk uninterrupted?"

"I'm a working woman. My day isn't over until well after six."

"But you've refused to have dinner with me—"

"Then I guess you're out of luck." She put her fingers to her temples to still the thudding that had settled there. "Besides, there's nothing to talk about. You looked familiar to me today in the restaurant. I stared at you. That's all. *Fini.*"

"Not quite. You still haven't told me how you know me. And you haven't given me a good reason why you won't go out with me."

Serena wanted to scream, but she internalized the urge along with the need to pound something. The gremlins within her head were doing that on their own. "Let's just say I don't like you," she mumbled.

"I know that. But I'd like to know why. What have I ever done to you? What have I ever done to deserve your disdain?"

"You really don't remember." Her statement reflected her disgust that what had meant so much to her family had meant nothing to him.

"No, I really don't remember. Why don't you make things easy for me?"

"Are you kidding? You'd like *me* to make things easy for *you?*" Furious, she went on. "Since when do *you* need help? Aren't you the all-powerful? All you have to do is to put your pen to paper and"—she snapped her fingers—"you've got what you want."

"Now, just a minute—"

"No. I think you should leave."

"I'm not going anywhere until I find out what you have against me!"

"Then I'll just call the police. You're trespassing . . . and causing a . . . disturbance. . . ."

They stood facing one another with only the counter between them. Tom's body was taut with anger; Serena trembled with the same. Both of their voices had been low, with the force of fire held in check. Now he spoke with the conviction she recalled so well.

"You won't call the police, Serena, because you really don't want to dredge up the past . . . whatever it is. . . ." His words trailed off lethally, leaving her a fragile mass of agony.

"You wouldn't. . . ." Her eyes widened; her head throbbed.

"I would."

Serena looked away, then swallowed hard. She believed him. He would have no qualms about destroying her life to find out what he wanted to know. Her whitened fingers curved around the edge of the counter as she slumped against a stool. Tom's voice jolted her, yet she couldn't look up.

"Monica!" he called toward the back. "Monica? Could you come out here, please?"

Within seconds Monica answered his summons. But it wasn't to Tom that her attention turned; rather, she stared at Serena's face, downcast and deathly pale.

Tom rounded the counter. "Monica, would you take care of things out here for a few minutes? I'm taking Serena out back. She's not feeling well." At Monica's look of alarm he reassured her quickly. "It's just a headache. But she could use a breather. Can you handle this?" His hand had already closed on Serena's arm; she felt too threatened to fight him.

"Sure. I'll take care of everything. Serena, are you sure you're all right? Can I call someone?"

"She'll be fine," Tom answered before Serena could answer for herself. "She's got me."

Feeling suddenly sick to her stomach, Serena yanked

her arm from his grasp and fled to the back room, where she rested against a tall carton, propping up her elbows and cradling her face on her fingertips. In her bid to escape she had missed the smile and accompanying wink Tom had sent toward Monica by way of mollification before he stepped confidently past her and followed Serena.

Assuming that she was witness to a lovers' spat, Monica was only too happy to respect their need to be alone. It was what she had sensed earlier, when she had diplomatically excused herself. Now they wanted more privacy. She could understand that. Cheeks flushed, she grew more starry eyed. Mr. whoever-he-was was very, very sexy!

Serena, however, was at the moment oblivious of any such charm. Head bowed, she struggled to regain control of the weakness in her stomach and the ache in her head. Breathing deeply, she feared she might even cry.

"Are you all right?" Tom's voice came more gently as his long fingers drew her hair back from her face.

She flinched and jerked away, unwittingly backing herself into a corner. The only positive aspect of the situation was the waist-high stepladder against which she was able to lean. Given the jelly-weakness of her knees, it was a minor blessing.

Tom stood over her, close enough for intimidation even as he spoke softly. His hands were thrust in the pockets of his slacks, his stance casual. Only the intensity in his eyes and the stubbornness underlying his quiet tone betrayed his tension.

"Now," he began, "you can start by reminding me of the first time we met." Serena wrapped both arms around her middle, looked down and said nothing. "Serena," he warned her.

"I'm not playing your games, Reynolds!" she whispered at last, not trusting her voice to remain steady if she spoke any louder. "You seem to know everything, despite that look of innocence you put on from time to time."

At the edge of her downcast field of vision his legs shifted. "Since you know so much about me, you also know that I'll carry out my threat. Would you like me to start searching through your past?"

She looked up slowly. "That's blackmail."

"You're *that* frightened of what you have to hide?"

"I have *nothing* to hide. You've got nothing on *me*. But I won't have you destroying my life now for something my father did years ago. He paid—we all paid!" Once more she dropped her eyes, closing them, lifting a hand to shade them from Tom's keen scrutiny.

His voice was lower, his words carefully chosen. "Tell me, in your own words, what your father did, Serena."

"You know. Why should I humiliate myself further?"

"Because"—his fingers took her chin and firmly raised it—"I want to hear you say it."

Serena tried to twist her head away, but the pounding got worse with the movement. "You must be sick!" she seethed.

"Say it. . . ." he warned again.

"What kind of pleasure can you get from this?"

"Serena, tell me about your father!"

She gritted her teeth. "I'll tell you as soon as you take your hand off me." For several moments they stared at one another. Then for the first time Tom yielded, dropping his hand, freeing her chin. It was an empty victory for Serena, for he took no more than a half step back, crossed his arms over his chest, and waited.

"Go on."

She took a shaky breath, propped herself once more against the ladder, and looked up defiantly. "My father was a good man. He loved his family and worked hard as an accountant. But he looked around and saw wealth on every side. And he was human. He made a mistake. You seized on that mistake as your stepping stone to success, capitalized on it, and made a public spectacle of my father." Her entire body trembled.

"What is your last name?" he asked softly.

"*What?*"

"Your last name—what is it?"

"My God!" she cried. "You don't even remember the name! Just how heartless are you, anyway?"

"The name, Serena. Tell me."

"Strickland! Strickland! My father was John Strickland. *Was.* He had a stroke several months after the conviction, while his lawyer was in the midst of the appeal process. It never went on. My father was paralyzed, spent weeks in the hospital, then three years in a nursing home before he died. Needless to say, life was just lovely for all of us during that period." Her note of sarcasm at the end did nothing to blunt the pure venom of her attack. But it left *her* writhing, rather than Tom.

To her dismay he stared at her as though she had risen from the dead. He seemed stunned. "Strickland," he said in an amazed whisper as his eyes covered every inch of her face. "Serena Strickland." Still he stared. "I remember your father so clearly, and your mother. There were two children, a boy and a girl. The boy was very young—"

"He was eight."

"And the girl wasn't much more than—"

"I was thirteen."

Tom continued as though in a daze, his brows drawn together with his frown. "She was kind of awkward, a little pudgy and very . . . very . . ."

"Vulnerable." Serena's breathing was uneven as she clung to her remaining self-control.

Astonished, he shook his dark head. "I can't believe you're the same girl!"

"I'm not," she snapped, shaking again. "And the hell I went through during those years had nothing to do with adolescence. Do you know what it's like to have friends whispering behind your back or suddenly avoiding you? It was as if I had the plague. I was 'daughter-of-the-thief'! Do you have *any idea* what that was like?" She paused for a breath, oblivious of the pained look spreading slowly across Tom's face. "No. Of course you don't. *You* never lived through anything like that. *You* are Thomas Harrison Reynolds of the illustrious Harrison publishing family. You never had to face the kind of disgrace you caused my father—"

"Serena," he cut in on a very quiet note, "I didn't tell him to steal."

"But you told everyone else *about it!*"

"I was a journalist. It was my job."

She tipped her head up in anger. "Now tell me you were only acting on orders."

"You know who I am." He threw her argument back in her face. "I don't follow orders."

"You were a young reporter then. It was your chance to hit it big on your own, is that it?"

"No."

"Then . . . what?" she cried more softly, feeling drained, tired, dizzy. Her headache had reached migraine proportions. "Why did you go after my father like that? Why . . . like that?"

Her voice died on a tremor that matched the shimmer of tears in her eyes. Tom's face blurred before her, his features blending in a dark cloud. Closing her eyes against further humiliation, she dropped her chin to her chest. Her shoulders rose and fell in her agitated attempt to stop short of an outright crying jag. Everything hurt so very badly.

"Let me get you something for that headache." Tom's voice was close above her and very gentle.

"It's all right," she whispered, knowing it wasn't.

"Have you got any aspirin?" She merely rocked back

47

and forth, trying to comfort herself. "Serena, don't you have a bottle of aspirin around?"

"Marshmallow," she croaked feebly, clamping her eyes more firmly shut against the nearness of this man who, by rights, was her enemy. Strangely, though, she couldn't fight any longer. Her fiery reaction to Tom had been out of character and she was too miserable now to persist.

Though he couldn't see her defeat, he sensed it clearly. Quite spontaneously he reached out, put his hands on her shoulders, then slid them around her back as he drew her to him. Serena went without a fight, too weary to reject his gesture of comfort. His identity was as unimportant as the fact that it was his presence that had caused her to get upset. The only reality was the pair of arms that steadied her and the warm body that absorbed her trembling.

Breathing deeply, Serena felt the slow return of strength to her limbs, but, reluctant to launch herself back into the fray, she made no attempt to move. Her cheek lay against his chest, her hands splayed on either side. Beneath her right hand his heart beat strongly, making him seem infinitely more human than he had in the heat of the fight.

Then, strangely, he was all too human. Suddenly she grew sharply aware of the strong length of his body, its strength barely concealed by the trappings of civilization. His clean, manly scent teased her with each breath she took. His chin rested on the crown of her head, threatening to hold her forever in this deceptively tranquil pose. He was a man to rest against . . . a man to lie against. . . .

With a gasp she pushed herself away, finding her legs as she fought the flush that threatened to betray her thoughts. "I—I think you should leave now," she whispered, pressing two fingers against the hammer behind her eyes.

"*I* think you should take something for that head-ache."

"It's a migraine. I used to get them all the time. It's been years since I've had one, though." She looked up at him. "You brought it on; perhaps if you leave it will go right along with you." The chances of that were slim, as past experience reminded her. It would, undoubtedly, be a bad night.

"Let me see you home."

"Is that the offer of a guilty conscience?"

"Not guilty. Perhaps pricked, but mostly sympathetic. You look as though you're in pain."

"An apt analysis," she muttered beneath her breath. "Perceptive."

"Come on." He ignored her sarcasm. "Get your things. I'll take you home."

"No, thank you. I can't leave until the shop closes. And that isn't for a while yet." As she recalled *Sweet Serenity* and what she'd made of it pride bolstered her. "I'll do just fine."

Tom stared at her a moment longer, his gaze express-ing his obvious skepticism. Finally he turned and left without a further word, at which point Serena became the skeptic. The next ninety minutes were excruciating. As she tried to function she pushed all thoughts of Tom Reynolds to a far corner of her mind. But from that corner he pounded at her head, growing more and more impatient, if the strength of her migraine was any in-dication.

Monica earned her pay three times over during that short space of time. She asked no questions, simply took over the handling of customers with the tact and self-assurance of a pro. And her boss was eternally grateful.

"Thanks, Monica." Serena forced a smile through her discomfort as they were closing up. "You've been terrific this afternoon. I'm not quite sure what I'd have done without you."

"I'll be back tomorrow." The teenager smiled. "If you feel like, you know, taking off for a while I'd be glad to cover."

"You're a dream"—Serena gave a genuine smile—"but I'll be here. This is my baby. There's nowhere I'd rather be."

The declaration referred to tomorrow. Right now, the only place she wanted to be was in bed under the weight of two quilts with the night cushioning her from the world. Senses dulled beneath the force of her headache, she stumbled through the last of the chores necessary after closing each day, threw her smart wool jacket on over her shoulders, grabbed her purse, knit hat and mittens, and made for the door. Blind to just about everything but her determination to get home in one piece, she turned her back on the plaza to lock and double-lock the door of *Sweet Serenity*. It was only when she turned back that, through the pain centered just above her eyes, she saw Tom.

3

He pushed off from his casual stance against the balustrade opposite her shop and stood no more than an arm's length away; she couldn't miss him.

"Oh, no," she murmured softly, taking a quick look at his face before averting her own.

"All ready to go?" he asked nonchalantly.

Bent on willing him out of existence, Serena stepped forward without a word, mechanically following the path she'd taken to and from work for the past five years. Beyond the blinders of her headache she was marginally aware of Tom keeping pace with her, but she was too miserable to argue. She paused only once, when she left the enclosure of the plaza and stepped into the cold night air, to button her coat to the throat, pull the thick wool hat over her ears and bury her shaking hands in the depths of her mittens.

"Cold night, isn't it?" Tom said with annoying light-heartedness, having stopped beside her to don and button the thigh-length, sheepskin-lined jacket that had been thrown over his arm.

Serena's grunt was as much at his company as his comment. But if she'd hoped he would take the hint that his presence wasn't wanted, she was disappointed. And she couldn't do anything to shake him, given the precarious state of her own health. It was enough to concentrate on putting one foot before the other, to combat the raging hammer in her head and the churning in her stomach. If the lights of the buildings on either side were excruciating to her vision, those of the oncoming cars were worse. When she pressed one mittened hand to her temple Tom grasped her other arm to steady her. Again she was too overwrought to protest.

What was in actuality no more than a ten-minute walk seemed a marathon to Serena. She thought she had never been as happy to see anything as she was when her apartment building came into view—then amended that at the relief she felt on finding herself on the fifteenth floor, at her own front door. She groped for the keys at the bottom of her bag, then fumbled with the lock until Tom took over the chore without a word. At that moment she could not care that he was on the threshold of her apartment. Her only thought was on getting to bed.

She was through the door and halfway across the living room without a backward glance when Tom switched on a light. Wincing, she shielded her eyes from its blinding glare, then reached the hall and finally her bedroom by sheer force of the momentum she'd established.

When she closed the bedroom door the noise reverberated through her. Stumbling forward, she pulled the curtains shut to blot out the lights of the city spread below her.

Darkness was a welcome friend. Slowly she shed her coat, hat and mittens, stepped out of her shoes, then one by one stripped the clothes from her body, draping the skirt and blouse on a chair, letting the rest fall haphazardly on the thick pile carpet underfoot.

A pair of slim bikini pants were all that was left as she stumbled to her bed, pulled back the covers and crawled beneath the heavy layers with a soft moan. The sheets soothed her; the dark enveloped her. With the quilts pulled to her ears she buried the worst of her migraine against the pillow. Her mind was a jumble of discomfort, with nausea coming and going in waves. As seconds passed into minutes and on toward an hour she sought nothing but the release of sleep.

Every so often she turned and burrowed more deeply into the bed, then moaned softly at the pain that persisted. The quiet sounds from her apartment—someone rummaging in the bathroom, the kitchen; a low voice on the telephone, at the door—failed to penetrate her door. Even if they had, she would have been deaf to them . . . or indifferent. The events of the afternoon had faded into a haze of pain. Nothing mattered to her but getting to sleep.

A widening sliver of light fell across the bed when the door opened. Serena was sufficiently buried beneath the covers to be undisturbed by the intrusion. When she was turned onto her back and bundled, covers and all, into a half-seated position, she squeezed her eyes shut.

"Go away," she whispered.

"Here, Serena. Take this."

"Aspirin won't help."

"It's your prescription."

"No! It's too old—"

"I know. I've just had a refill delivered."

"Oh—"

He handed her a small white pill and a glass of water, holding her steady as she took the medicine.

"OK?" he asked, taking the glass from her lips and putting it down on the night table by her bed.

Her echoed "OK" was barely audible.

53

Easing her gently back on the bed, Tom sat for a minute, then stood and left, drawing the door tightly closed, leaving her alone once more in her cocoon of darkness. Almost instantly she began to feel better, though the medication could not possibly have worked so quickly. Later, somewhere in her mind, came the soothing vision of a warm hand on the bare skin of her back, a strong arm supporting her, long fingers stroking wayward strands of hair from her cheeks. The sensations were very real, their pleasantness lingering to bring her relief until the time when the medicine entered her bloodstream and went to work. Then she fell into a deep and restorative sleep, awakening once very much later to walk to the bathroom for another pill and set her alarm before falling quickly asleep again. When she awoke the second time it was morning.

Despite the deep sleep induced by the medication, her alarm had not yet rung. Groggy, she sat up, blinked, stretched, pushed the hair back out of her eyes. She felt decidedly better. The residual ghost of her headache would ease now with a dose of aspirin. The nausea was already long gone.

Slipping from bed, she donned a robe and stepped into slippers, took fresh underwear from the drawer, and headed for a hot shower. It felt divine. Turning slowly, she soaped herself, applied a generous helping of shampoo to her wet hair, rinsed off the lot, then stood. And stood. Turning occasionally. Letting the water cascade over her gentle curves. Repositioning herself to let the steaming spray hit her neck, her back, her chest, her shoulders. It was only when she began to feel immoral at her lavish use of hot water that she reluctantly stemmed the flow.

The heat of the shower had warmed the fluffy towel that lay in waiting across its rack. With a definite sense of pampering herself she reached for it and patted the water from her body before treating it to a helping of scented moisture lotion. She wrapped the towel around herself, then vigorously rubbed her hair with a smaller towel before brushing through the tangles. It was only then, as she stared into the mirror at the reflection of her pale though recuperating self, that she allowed herself to think of Tom.

Tom Reynolds. The devil of her memory. The uninvited visitor to her shop yesterday. The inquisitor. The cause of her migraine headache. Then . . . the self-appointed guardian who had seen her safely home. The silent protector. The gentle caretaker. All in all, a potpourri of conflicting characteristics. Who *was* Tom Reynolds?

Her gaze grew puzzled as she noticed the new bottle of medicine that he had had the presence of mind to order. Why had he waited outside *Sweet Serenity* last night? Why his insistence on walking her home? Why had he bothered to see to the medicine and make sure she was sound asleep before leaving? It made no sense.

Shaking off the last of her fogginess, she faced the future. It was a new day. She felt vastly improved. And she would *not,* she vowed, be driven to another headache by Thomas Harrison Reynolds. Seeing him yesterday had been a shock which she was now over, although there remained the matter of her past, which he had recalled. Intuitively she sensed that he wouldn't betray her, though she knew that, for her own peace of mind, she would eventually have to confront him about it. She'd have to know for certain that her life in Minneapolis would be safe from the taint of the past. But that would be for another time, should their paths cross again. For now, there was the day to welcome.

It was a relatively steady hand that applied her make-up, working more carefully with color around eyes dulled by last night's headache, adding a bit more blusher than usual to still-pale cheeks. She stroked through her hair with a natural bristle brush, bringing up a fine luster, pushing willful curls this way and that until she was satisfied with the results. Then, encouraged by the normality of her appearance, she set out for a cup of hot, strong coffee.

Her apartment was small but well-planned. Its single bedroom and bath opened off a hallway from the living room. The kitchen had two open archways, one opposite the bedroom, the other leading directly into the living room. It was through the first that she entered, humming softly to herself. The fresh, dark brew was dripping into the pot within minutes. Its aroma never failed to please her. Smiling, she savored its richness, then headed for the living room and the *Tribune* that would be on the mat outside her front door.

She managed to set only one slippered foot into the living room. Then she gasped. For rising slowly to a sitting position on the sofa, his back to her, was the figure of a man. She had no idea that he'd spent the night; the thought hadn't entered her mind. Yet there before her was a sleep-disheveled, very groggy Tom Reynolds.

His back was a broad expanse of white shirt; his dark head was bent forward. Serena stared, fascinated, as he put a hand to his neck to massage away the cricks that her sofa had undoubtedly planted. His fingers worked at his taut muscles and he stretched to relieve the stiffness.

Her eye followed the manly ritual, yet she was touched by something totally non-physical. Unobserved as he thought he was, he seemed utterly human and very vulnerable. Despite his great status, he was prone to the same aches and pains as the next man. And he was here, in her apartment . . . still. Why?

She emerged slowly from the doorway to walk hesitantly around the sofa, pausing in front of it when Tom looked up, sending a momentary quiver through her. Yesterday he had been immaculate in his appearance and handsome; now he was tired, his chin shadowed by a beard, seemingly at a disadvantage. Seemingly, yet not. For he was still more attractive, crumpled shirt, heavy eyes and all, than any other man she had ever known.

"Good morning," she heard herself announce softly and quite civilly.

Tom looked dubious and sounded even more so. "Umm. Is that smell what I think it is?" He raked his fingers through his hair as he shot a glance toward the kitchen.

"Uh-huh. Would you like a cup?"

"'Like' has little to do with it. 'Need' is more the issue." In one surprisingly fluid movement he was off the sofa and headed toward the kitchen. "If you'll excuse me . . ."

Serena quirked an auburn brow at his grumpiness, smiled, then followed through on her original intention. When she returned to the kitchen with the paper in hand she paused on the threshold, this time with a note of trepidation. After all, she wasn't sure why Tom was still here. And nothing was worth another headache.

Reading her thoughts, he looked up from the coffee cup he'd found and filled. "How are you feeling?"

"Better."

"You slept well?"

"Yes."

"The pills helped?"

"Uh-huh. And . . . thank you." She looked down, unsure for a moment. "I'm not sure I could have done *anything* last night, let alone think about getting a refill on my prescription."

He shrugged, standing up to lean against the counter by the sink. "It was the least I could do." His eyes were unreadable.

Standing awkwardly by the door, Serena wasn't quite sure what to do. It seemed to be a recurrent ailment when Tom was around. Finally her own need drove her toward the cabinet, a cup, and some coffee. "I'll repay you for whatever you spent on the pills," she offered without looking up.

"That won't be necessary."

"I'd prefer it."

"I said it won't be necessary." Draining his coffee, he helped himself to more.

But if his insistence was due to early morning testiness, Serena's was based on principle. Despite the fact that Tom had been the instigating factor behind her migraine, she wanted to owe him nothing. "If you'll just tell me what it came to I'll pay you. I don't like being indebted to anyone."

"Especially me?"

Her direct gaze held a challenge. "To *anyone*."

Tom studied her through less hazy eyes. "A legacy?"

"If you will."

"It's not necessary in this case, you know." He spoke more gently in response to her vehemence. "We're only talking about a couple of dollars. And since I was responsible for upsetting you it makes me feel better knowing that I've been able to aid in your recovery." His hazel eyes flicked quickly over her. "You do look better. Is the headache gone?"

"Pretty much. I'll take some aspirin before I leave for work. It'll be fine."

But he was skeptical. "Considering how sick you were last night, I would have thought you'd stay in bed, at least for the morning."

"I can't do that," she answered softly. "*Sweet Serenity* is *my* responsibility. If I don't get there to open it up it doesn't open."

"What about your help—that young girl I saw yesterday?"

"Monica comes in after school. I do have another woman who works mornings for me, but she has a family and can't get away in time to open the shop."

58

"What if you were *really* sick? Isn't there anyone who can take over for you?"

Serena answered him calmly. "Fortunately I've never *been* really sick, so the matter hasn't been put to the test." She looked away more pensively. "And even if I was unable to open for a day, the world would survive."

Her philosophical quip wafted into a small eternity of silence. Neither said a word. As the seconds ticked away she thought of the man who stood with her in her kitchen. Never would she have imagined him here. Indeed, one part of her wanted to be angry at him, to denounce him scathingly, to oust him from her apartment, from her life. Yet she somehow couldn't seem to translate the thought into action. Instead she simply stared at his rangy form as he lounged against the counter.

He stared back. His features were deceptively calm, masking the thoughts that swirled within. But the fire was there in his gaze, tempered, but refusing to be overlooked. By instinct Serena knew that she was his focal point. She grew suddenly and uncomfortably aware of the simple wrap robe she was wearing and tugged it more tightly around her.

"Would you—would you like some breakfast?" she finally stammered when she could stand the silence no longer.

His brow arched. "You'd really cook me breakfast?"

"Of course." She frowned, pausing. "You seem . . . surprised. I *do* know how to cook."

A snort of amusement preceded his explanation. "That's not the point, Serena. You weren't exactly thrilled to see me yesterday. And I'm sure you never planned on having me spend the night in your apartment. I am, after all," he drawled facetiously, "the enemy. Am I not?"

Intentionally or otherwise, he had summarized her

quandary. "I suppose so. . . ." But she was unable to hide her puzzlement.

Tom noted it and went on. "So it's natural for me to be surprised that you're offering me breakfast."

"Perhaps I feel that I owe it to you. For the pills and the care, and all," she rationalized off the top of her head.

"And all." He smiled sadly. "I really didn't do very much."

"You were here," she blurted out unthinkingly, then swallowed the revealing words that might have followed.

Their eyes met as they recalled the same moments. A hand on her back. Fingers stroking her hair. Arms supporting her. The solace of a human presence. Serena was overwhelmed by confusion, trying desperately to remember who he was, all the while feeling herself drawn to him.

"Look—" she began, only to be interrupted.

"Tom. The name's Tom."

"Tom." It fell softly, for the first time, from her tongue. "What would you like?"

Straightening, he took several steps toward her, then stopped. His gaze grew more sensual, falling to her lips in a visual caress that shimmered through her newly awakening body. Suspended in time and unreality, she couldn't move.

Tom opened his mouth to speak, then thought better of it and clamped his lips together, only to take a breath and begin again seconds later. "I'd like to clean up a little, if you don't mind. Then some eggs, toast, whatever, will do."

"Sunny-side up?"

"Over easy."

"Butter on the toast?"

"Jam, please."

"Orange juice?"

"Tomato will be fine."

"Wow! You really *did* go through my refrigerator last

night. It's not everyone who keeps a full stock of tomato juice." She looked at him askance. "What kind of jam?"

Though he feigned timidity there was no hesitation in his response. "Wild plum? . . ."

She mocked disgust. "Hmph. You'd even ask for my prize possession."

"There's plenty in the jar—"

"You've already looked *inside?*"

"Well"—he threw his head back—"I *was* here all evening. I was hungry." He smiled.

Serena flew to the refrigerator, extracted the decorative jam jar, and analyzed its contents. "You didn't make a meal of wild plum jam, did you?"

"Actually," he drawled on his way toward the bathroom, "it was dessert—atop a couple of crackers."

"And the main course?" she called after him.

"That jar of herring in wine sauce did the trick."

"My herring in wine sauce?" she cried, aghast. She'd been saving it for a special occasion, some night when she felt the need for a treat. Now Tom had devoured it whole. "You didn't!" She followed him to the hall, only to find herself face to face with the bathroom door.

Slowly it opened. "I did." Smiling pleasantly, Tom stood before her, leisurely unbuttoning his shirt, then pulling it out of his pants. Serena momentarily forgot the point of her chase. The sight of him standing there, tall and straight, at her bathroom door, his face shadowed in sensuality, his chest firm and manly, drove prudence from mind. He was the enemy, yet from the start he had embodied a fire that captivated her. In the restaurant yesterday it had been a fire from the past; here and now it held no memory. It was new and unsullied, a spark of wonder that flared from him with breathtaking intensity. Its heat consumed her antagonism even as it inspired cravings Serena would have refused to believe had she not felt the warmth that suddenly flowed through her veins.

Enthralled by his nearness and the effect of his virility, she felt a tug from deep within, willing her forward, urging her fingers to touch what he had so knowingly laid bare. Unsure of everything but the force of the attraction she tore her gaze from the matted richness sprawled beneath his shirt and sought his eyes.

In an instant he closed the short distance between them and stood no more than a breath away. Serena's breath caught in her throat. The push she had felt moments before from within was now a summons from Tom, a call from his manliness to her womanhood, a primal note she had never in her wildest dreams expected and against which she had no defense.

Tom lifted his hand to her face, gently threading his fingers through the damp tendrils of her auburn hair, softly caressing the creamy smoothness of her cheek, planting new images and fresh sensations with every stroke. On instinct she tipped her head to his palm, all the while unable to take her eyes from his. He seemed as mesmerized as she by the moment; all was irrelevant save the two of them. He searched the depths of her gaze as she explored his. And then, slowly and inevitably, he lowered his head by fractions of inches until his lips very lightly touched hers.

Serena was entranced, having lost all touch with reality under the onslaught of this man's sensuality. She felt his mouth as it sampled the soft curve of her lips, whispering a kiss at each corner. The musky scent of his skin drugged her further, sending her reeling into a world of sensation. Had his free arm not surrounded her and drawn her close against him she would have fallen. Her limbs trembled beneath the unexpected attack, and a sweet attack it was.

From the start her defenses had been down. She was a woman with a core of passion that had long lain dormant. Tom Reynolds had struck the match and now warmed her with it. His lips were firm, yet gentle, coaxing hers to open to his repeated forays. As for Serena, she was beyond rational decision. When her lips finally parted in longing there was nothing rational about it. She was driven by desire, strong and pure.

Tom welcomed her kiss with a joy transmitted by the tremor of his body when he clutched her more closely. He held her head to explore her lips, running the tip of his tongue along her teeth before plunging further. Serena could only quiver at the heady invasion and respond in kind, opening her mouth further in invitation, freeing her own tongue to exact passionate retribution.

Somewhere along the line her arms found their way beneath his shirt to his back. En route her fingers savored the firmness of his flesh, its rough man-texture so much in contrast to her own silken skin. She was delirious at the difference, gasping into his mouth at the feel of his body as he pressed her to him. He was warm, strong and hard, his friction kindling tiny fires at every touchpoint. And they were both still dressed. . . .

As though reading her thoughts and sensing their direction Tom drew back to frame her face with his hands. Slowly she opened her eyes.

"You'd only hate me more." He spoke thickly, his breath coming in uneven gasps that matched hers. It took Serena longer to recover from the trance of arousal he'd inspired. At her puzzled frown he explained, laboring as he struggled to contain his own primitive heat.

"You hate me for the past, Serena." His eyes circled her face, pausing to appreciate each feature. "But there's a flame between us that isn't just destructive. I only know I want you. I've wanted you since I first saw you yesterday afternoon, when I had no idea who you were, only sensed that you felt very strongly about me." His thumbs caressed the back of her neck, his fingers crept across her cheeks toward her mouth in helpless wandering. "You're very lovely," he rasped, dipping his head to touch her lips a final time. Serena was all too eager to return, if only for the instant, to that mindless state of sensual excitement. But it was too brief. And Tom was determined to remind her of who she was, of who *he* was.

He was more strongly in control when he spoke again. "I couldn't sleep last night, having held you in my arms like that. Do you know what it does to a man to find the woman he wants in bed, naked?"

For the first time it dawned on Serena that her action might easily have been interpreted as a lure. "I'm sorry." She shook her head. "I didn't realize. I always sleep like that and I was sure you would leave."

"I didn't. I couldn't."

She had no answer for him. What could she say? There was so much to be considered, so much to be worked out in her mind, before she could try to explain her emotions. To make matters worse, with each passing moment the enormity of what she'd craved just now crowded in on her. Tom tuned in to her dilemma.

"You see?" He set her back just out of reach, dropping his arms limply to his sides. "We could have made love. . . ." As his words trailed off he stared once more, long and hard, at her expression of slow-growing horror, then turned and shut himself in the bathroom again.

As though rooted to the hardwood floor Serena stood, stunned, appalled, confused. It was only the gentle reminder at her temple, the soft throbbing echo of yesterday's headache, that finally freed her from the spot and turned her toward the kitchen. When Tom emerged from the bathroom ten minutes later she had regained a semblance of composure. Nothing had been resolved; the situation hadn't changed. But for the moment she was unable to do anything about it, and making breakfast seemed the only plausible course of action.

"You showered and shaved?" She looked up in surprise at his well-groomed visage as he entered.

Tom grinned. "I hope you don't mind, I helped myself to your things. There's nothing worse than feeling grubby."

"You had enough hot water?" She thought of the indecently long shower she'd taken not terribly long ago.

"*Hot* water wasn't what I wanted. Except for the shave. And the last of the shower. *After* the cold water had done its thing." The mischief in his eye did *its* thing, stirring Serena afresh. "But, yes, I had enough hot water for my needs. Thank you."

Serena shrugged, then turned silently to put the eggs and toast on a plate, which she handed to him. Then she reached for the coffee. She kept her eyes averted, refusing to let his physical appeal blow her mind again. It was only after she'd slid onto the chair opposite his that she dared to look at him again.

"Mmmm, these eggs are just right," he said, ignoring the tension between them.

"You really didn't remember me, did you?" Serena refused to evade the issue.

"Any salt?"

"Tom . . ."

"The salt?"

She sighed in defeat and reached for the shaker. She watched him sprinkle the salt on his eggs, then start eating again. After several mouthfuls he looked up in surprise.

"You're not eating?" he asked innocently.

"I have toast," she said with a glance to her plate, "and coffee. That's all I ever have."

"Not healthy."

"Neither is salt."

"Touché." He returned to the serious business of eating, undaunted by her claim.

"I didn't even call your bluff." She took a different tack, shaking her head in self-disgust. "You were just fishing for information and I gave it to you."

"You were upset. I'm sure that you're usually much sharper."

"Oh? Now why would you be so sure?" she prodded.

"I looked at you. Your shop. Your apartment. Your life. You must be a very efficient—and sharp—lady to manage everything on your own."

"A person does certain things because she has no other choice."

"You didn't have to open a shop of your own. You could have chosen to go through life without that responsibility."

She held his gaze more confidently. "*Sweet Serenity* means a lot to me. I need it."

"And you've made a success of it, which makes my point. If you had nothing on the ball"—he tapped his head—"the shop would have folded long ago."

Serena nibbled absently on her toast. "Tom, why *did* you come to the store yesterday? If you honestly didn't make the connection between the past and me, why did you come?"

"I told you that yesterday. You intrigued me. I wanted to find out who you were."

"And now that you know," she said uneasily, "what do you intend to . . . to do with that information?"

"With what information?" He seemed genuinely puzzled.

"The Strickland connection."

He looked at her as though she were warped. "Absolutely nothing! Is there something I *should* be doing with it?" When Serena didn't reply but merely looked away, he put down his fork. "Serena, that's ancient history. It's a closed book. *You* seem to be the only one aware of any 'Strickland connection.'"

Her gaze shot back to his. "Not exactly."

"What do you mean?"

"I mean," she spoke quietly, tempering the hurt that still lingered, "that some information has a way of finding itself in the wrong people's hands. It's happened before and it could happen again."

"Explain." He rested his chin in the crook between his thumb and forefinger, stroking his jaw thoughtfully.

Suddenly realizing that she had opened up much more than she'd wanted to, she demurred. "Never mind; you were right. It's past history."

But Tom wouldn't let her off the hook. "Finish what you've begun, Serena. What happened?"

Strangely, Tom was the first person to know enough about her past for her to speak freely about the pain of it. Even more strangely, she heard herself telling him about Michael Lowry.

"When I was a senior in high school—I was living with an aunt and uncle in New York at the time—I became involved with a fellow." Her voice lowered with her eyes. "He was in college. Older. More worldly. From a prominent family."

"That mattered to you?"

"No! I couldn't have cared less! But it mattered to *him*. *He* let me know in no uncertain terms just how prominent his family was."

"What happened?"

She hesitated, feeling awkward. It was only the compassion on Tom's face that gave her the courage to continue. "As I said, we became involved. It went on for several months. I had been accepted at Duke University, but I wasn't sure I wanted to leave him. So . . . I confronted him about it."

"You wanted him to marry you?"

"No, not really. I just wanted him to give me some indication of his feelings. If he had felt that we might marry one day I would have gone to school in New York."

"And . . . ?"

Again she paused, frowning at her clenched hands, swallowing convulsively. This time it was the sight of Tom's hand and its warmth enveloping hers that buoyed her. "He made it very clear that he could . . . *never* marry me. After all," she mimicked Michael's long-ago statement of what he saw as the obvious, "what with my family history, his parents would never have even considered the match."

Tom's body stiffened as his hand tightened over hers. "He was using you all that time?"

"No, I can't really say that." Her gaze was sad but sincere. "We both enjoyed the relationship. He never made any promises. It was me—me who needed the reassurance—me who needed the . . ."

". . . love?"

Her soft-whispered "perhaps" was another beginning. "It had been a very lonely time for me. Once I left California I needed someone to take the place of my family. Oh, I had my aunt and uncle, but there was something strange about their attitude toward me. I've never been able to figure them out—they seemed torn between duty and conscience. They were warm and caring enough, but I can't go so far as to say that they loved me." She shrugged off that particular hurt. "At any rate, Michael filled a need. I thought he loved me. I guess I was simply imagining much more than there was."

For a time there was silence. Tom stood to pour them each more coffee, put the pot back on its warmer, walked to the window, then returned to where Serena sat. "That has to be over ten years ago. Were there any other incidents?"

Serena's laugh held a wealth of bitterness. "You can be sure I never put myself in that position again."

"You haven't been with a man since?"

She ignored the implication. "I haven't looked for anything more than an evening's fun."

"A *night*'s fun?"

"An evening's fun." She sighed. "No, Tom, I sleep alone. That avoids a lot of pain."

"It also rules out fulfillment."

Threatened anew, she looked away. "I fill my life with . . . other things."

"Is that why you responded to me the way you did a little while ago?"

"Tom . . ." she protested.

"No, Serena, don't stop me. You opened up to me as a very passionate woman. Can you really keep all that stopped up inside?"

"I don't."

"But you just implied . . ."

"No, I don't sleep around. But I don't suffer from pent-up frustration, either. Much as you men would like to believe that every single woman could have all her problems cured by a man, it just isn't so."

"I should hope not." He sipped his coffee slowly, absently. "But the passion's there, Serena. In you. Maybe not for just any man. But it's there for me."

"No," she lied, unwilling to face that fact herself.

Tom didn't push her on it. "Let me ask you something." He hesitated for a moment to gather his thoughts. "Why have you told me all this—about that guy in New York and all?"

Lashing out in self-defense, Serena grew more tense. "Perhaps I wanted you to know some of what I went through as a result of what you did."

"So we're back to that?"

"Always! When I see your face," she lied again, "I see the man who was responsible for all the torment my family suffered. Oh, I know it was my father who

69

committed the crime. You don't have to remind me of that. But you were the one who exposed him so cruelly. You were the one who put him on the front page. You were the one who publicized his error. You were the one who magnified the humiliation for *all* of us!" In her anguish she bolted from the chair and stormed into her bedroom, slamming the door behind her much as she had done last night, though this time not seeking darkness. On the contrary, it was the light she sought. Reality. Awareness. It was all too easy to forget what Tom Reynolds had done to her family. In his arms it was all too easy to forget everything.

"Serena?"

Whirling around, she found him in her room, not an arm's length away. "Please, Tom. Enough's been said. I've got to get dressed and get to the shop. Please leave."

"All right, Serena. I don't want to upset you. Believe me, it gave me no pleasure to see what I'd done to you last night. But I want you to know that I'm not giving up." Suddenly his quiet air took on an edge.

Her eyes widened fearfully. "What are you talking about?"

"You and me. I didn't spend the whole of last night on your sofa just to wake up this morning, say goodbye, and walk out of your life."

"You have to."

"I don't have to do anything. And"—his gaze narrowed—"I don't think you really want me to vanish."

"Yes I do!"

"Do you?" He tipped his head in skepticism. "Can you deny what happened before? Wouldn't you like to follow it through, to see where it will lead?"

"No!" she whispered on the fragment of a breath.

His hands came down firmly on her shoulders, holding her still when she might have run from him. "Listen to me, Serena." He spoke more softly. "I've been burned, too. My life hasn't been the song and dance you'd like to believe. I've had my share of heartache. And, to be perfectly honest, I don't know what the hell I'm doing telling all this to you. But I spent last night fighting the frustration of wanting you and not knowing why. And if there's one thing I've learned in my business it's that when a hot tip comes in I owe it to myself to follow it. I'm going to follow this one, Serena. It may be a dead end. But somewhere in my gut I have a feeling . . ."

"No!" she murmured in a half-cry, slowly shaking her head.

"Yes. I'll see it through."

Serena tried to pull away from him, but his grip merely tightened. "No . . . no . . ." He was close and alluring; the battle was now within herself.

"Serena," he moaned with an agony that stilled her. Again she felt herself falling under his spell. "Serena . . ."

He caught her lips quickly, as though afraid she'd fight. But the devil within her had taken temporary advantage, stirring up her need to the exclusion of reason. His clean scent pervaded her being; his body offered its protection; his lips consumed hers with a hunger that surmounted the purely physical. Serena fought to stay above the tide of passion, but its force quickly overpowered her and, with a soft cry from the back of her throat, she yielded to its drive and was lost.

Or was she? Was this surrender, or victory? Defeat, or discovery? Once more Tom's seductive prowess flooded her with delight, drowning any resistance she might have intended to make. Was she weak in capitulation, or strong in the height of the passion he evoked so easily? It was raw pleasure she felt at his touch, and she thrilled to it.

Eager to explore the glory of her womanhood, she wound her arms over his shoulders and around his neck, thrusting her fingers through the fullness of his hair as she urged him closer. Tom sensed the change and his fierceness eased, calming to a more seductive exploration of her mouth, her eyes, her cheeks. His tongue found her ear and traced its intricacies, sending ripples of excitement from one cell to the other.

Serena glowed, blooming beneath the nourishment of his affection. She reveled in his care, savored his appreciation, all the while seeking more and more from him. Her lips explored the rougher texture of his skin, kissing, nipping, tasting his unique flavor while her hands discovered his manly shape.

The sounds of the morning were gentle ones, soft sighs and breathy moans of delight. When Tom swung around and sat on the edge of her bed she was drawn to him still, held between the strength of his thighs with her arms draped over his shoulders.

"Mmm, Serena," he rasped, trailing the fire of his tongue from her ear to her neck and into the hollow of her throat. She pressed the flush of her cheek against his hair, holding him against her, wanting this joy to continue. Long ago, in another's arms, she had known the pleasures of love, but there was something different now. There was maturity behind it all, a finer realization of the pinnacle of ecstasy to be shared between a man and a woman. Suddenly she wanted to see it through. Suddenly she needed to assuage the taut yearning at her core.

"Yes, Tom," she whispered in a haze of passion as she arched instinctively toward him. She framed his face and tipped it up, lowering her own to kiss him with the heat of the fire that flamed from within. As his mouth covered hers his fingers found the tie to her robe, easily releasing it, pushing the soft fabric aside, trembling as he spanned the flesh of her waist then moved upward.

"Ahhh," Serena whimpered, acutely aware of the throbbing knot inside. "Oh, Tom . . ."

Her breasts swelled beneath his touch, filling the hand that covered the delicate lace of her bra. The finger that slid within had the gentle roughness of a cat's tongue, driving her to distraction as it worked its way to a pebbled crest tipped with rose. Again she called his name, wanting him, needing him, aching for more than the demands of the morning would allow.

Her impassioned trance was so thick that she wasn't aware of his tension until his hoarse-muttered "Damn it" tore through her. "Damn it," he growled a second time, more vehemently now and with the intent of distracting himself from the love-play that was nearly out of hand.

Gasping for breath, Serena allowed herself to be pushed away. "Tom?"

"Damn it! I don't want this!" he fairly screamed. *"I won't do this!"*

His face was a sudden mask of anger, terrifying Serena. "What is it?" she asked, frantic. But he wouldn't say anything more. Instead he pushed himself from the bed, headed for the door and disappeared toward the living room, leaving her a shaky melange of desire, frustration, and outright perplexity. "Tom?" she called a final time, but quietly, because something held her back. When she finally dared to venture from her room and searched the apartment he was gone.

Dazed, she returned to her room and sank into her Bentwood rocker, moving absently back and forth to the rhythm of defeat. As it slowly circled the room her eye fell on the clothes she'd discarded so carelessly last night, the bed still mussed from her drugged sleep, the family photo atop her dresser. Despite what he had done to her in the past, and whatever his motives for leaving had been just now, Serena was grateful to Tom for his exit. He'd been only partly right earlier, she mused sadly. For not only would she have hated him had he taken her, as she had all but begged him to do, she would have hated herself forever. And *that* would have been, by far, the worst.

As it was Tom could—and would, if his parting words meant what she thought they had—disappear from her life for good. And she had somehow to cope with the self-disgust she felt at having totally surrendered to the charm of him, her sworn enemy. But had the farce been seen through—*that* would have been tragic.

With an initial stop in the bathroom for the aspirin she had promised herself earlier Serena forced all thoughts of Tom from her mind as she cleaned the apartment, dressed, and headed for the shop. She opened on time, with no one to know what had happened during those nighttime hours. Only Serena knew. Only Serena remembered . . . against her wishes. Only Serena trembled in hindsight. And only Serena understood when, shortly after noon, the florist delivered a small bouquet of delicate baby roses, a spray of pert pink petals in a bed of bright greenery. The brilliant white of its message card reached out to her; driven by an emotion she refused to analyze she reached for it almost with eagerness.

"To sweet Serena," she read. *"Perhaps one day you'll forgive me. Tom."*

The script was firm and bold, much as the man behind it. Was this a farewell he'd sent? she wondered through the afternoon as her gaze brushed the fragrant bouquet time and time again. If so, it was surely for the best. She had her life, her friends, and *Sweet Serenity*. Tom had his papers and the power they gave him. Their lives ran in opposite directions, their backgrounds even more so. She liked her eggs sunny-side up; he preferred his over easy.

She frowned. But what about wild plum jam? And

herring in wine sauce? And the heat of passion un-
leashed?

Then, that very evening, she learned of another shared
love when she arrived at the racquetball club to find none
other than Thomas Harrison Reynolds, devastatingly
masculine in shorts and a jersey, ready to serve his
partner from the far end of Court One.

4

~~~~~~~~~~~~

To Serena's chagrin she and Cynthia were slotted for Court Five, directly across the way and within clear sight of the match just beginning on Court One.

"Pretty clever." Cynthia smiled, coming from behind to startle her from her trance. "Did you arrange to meet here? Have plans for dinner later?"

"No!" Serena exclaimed. "I had no idea he'd be here."

"You two did work things out though, didn't you?"

"Uh . . . not exactly."

Serena's vagueness captured her friend's curiosity. "What does that mean, 'not exactly'? This is very mysterious. I love it!"

"Don't." Serena frowned. "There's nothing mysterious about it. Actually, there's nothing about it at all."

"You mean that you haven't made your play yet?"

"I mean that I don't intend to make a play."

"Serena! I'm crushed. How can you let such a prime sample of masculinity slip right through your fingers?"

"Very easily."

Serena let it go at that as the two women stood watching the progress on Tom's court. She noticed that he was a skilled player. In fact, she would give her right hand to play with him.

"Who is he, anyway?" Cynthia broke into her thoughts once more.

"His name is Tom Reynolds."

"Tom Reynolds." The redhead tapped her lips with the lacquered tip of one tapered fingernail. "Tom Reynolds . . . where have I heard that name before?"

Serena saw no point in secrecy. After all, Tom's identity was public information. "He's the new owner of the *Bulletin*."

"You're kidding! *That* owns the newspaper?"

"*That* does."

"And you'd blow a chance to be with him?"

"I'm not blowing anything, Cynthia," Serena calmed her friend. "We just have our differences."

"Racquetball isn't one of them."

"Umm."

"Did you know he played here?"

"I didn't know he played, period. That should tell you something about our relationship."

"I'm all ears." Her friend smiled coaxingly.

But Serena had never been one to confide deeply in others, particularly about such personal matters. "I'll bet." She smiled back, but shut her mouth firmly by way of delivering her message. She never knew whether Cynthia received it, for the other woman's attention was glued to the action opposite them.

"He's good," Cynthia murmured with a touch of awe.

A deep voice responded, drawing both women's attention momentarily away from the game. "He *should* be! He was the fifth ranked player in the country a while back. He was instrumental in establishing racquetball as a going sport."

77

Cynthia was the first to recover. "And how do *you* know so much about him, Willie?"

"I work here, doll. He's been in several times a week for the past month. Just moved to the area. I'd say we're pretty lucky. Could be that he'll spice things up around here!"

Serena's laugh erupted spontaneously and held its share of sarcasm. "Could be," she echoed tartly. "He's a born agitator." The instant she spoke she caught her breath. That was what André had said just yesterday, when they had seen Tom in the restaurant, when neither of them had known who he was. Sixteen years ago he had earned the label. Did it still apply? What he had done to her yesterday and that morning added up to a more private form of agitation. What *was* he like as a person?

"He's good!" Cynthia repeated her earlier exclamation, to be echoed by Willie once again.

"I'll say! He doesn't compete anymore, but he sure could beat the pants—pardon me, ladies—off anybody here!"

At that point, bidden by some unknown force, Tom looked up and focused on them. Cynthia nudged Serena, whose pulse tripped dangerously even without the reminder that Tom had seen her. When he finally turned back to play all eyes were on him. His opponent served, he returned a ceiling ball; his opponent slammed a kill shot to the corner—and Tom missed.

Serena turned on her heel, having seen enough. The image was all too fresh in her mind—long, muscled arms and legs, a natural grace amid the speed of the game, an undeniable mastery of the sport itself—and did even less for her concentration than her presence had done for Tom's. Had it not been for his obvious skill and the information Willie had freely offered, she might have wondered if his presence was something short of coincidence. But he was a pro—and he had been as stunned to see her as she was to see him.

Serena felt no satisfaction at having distracted Tom. When Cynthia teased her, she came to his defense.

"Wow! You sure shake *him* up!"

"Not quite, Cyn. He was just surprised, that's all. Willie was right; I'm sure he'll beat the pants off that guy!"

She didn't linger to watch the outcome of the game, but dragged her friend toward their own court. Her play was far below par, though. And Cynthia noted that, as well, commenting on it when the hour was up.

"Boy, you two better get it together or you'll both be kicked out of the club," she teased. "Better still, we'll put you on a court together and you can stand there looking at each other. If nobody serves the ball, nobody misses."

"Cynthia, have pity on me," Serena gasped, collapsing on the sidelines while the redhead collected her things.

"He's gone, at any rate."

"Oh?"

"As if you didn't know."

Serena *did* know. She knew at precisely what point he had finished, precisely how long he had followed the activity on Court Five, and precisely which men he'd spoken to as he headed for the locker room. It was no wonder her own game was shot, she'd barely been aware of what she was doing!

Moments later the two women headed for their own locker room. "Listen, Serena, if you're not interested in him, I'll be glad—"

"Thanks, but I'll let you know," Serena interrupted, not sure what she was talking about, though her words sounded full of confidence. In fact, she was sure of nothing, except the fact that she could *not* turn Cynthia loose on Tom. Not that she had any claim on him herself, or *wished* to have any, nor that *he* had serious designs on her, but she was simply not ready to make any definitive judgment where Tom Reynolds was concerned. There was still that spark he lit in her, a spark no other man in recent years had ignited. Granted, she'd let no man get as close as Michael Lowry had been—for the very reason for which he'd scorned her. But Tom knew about that past; he'd said it didn't matter. Could she ever see eye to eye with him on that score?

As the days passed Serena wondered often about Tom. He was a link to her past, a potentially devastating one, yet she didn't feel threatened as she had at first. She trusted him in some strange way, though the "why" of it eluded her. Much as she felt guilty at the aggressive behavior she'd shown that morning in her apartment, she couldn't squelch the curiosity she felt—any more than she could the remembered tingle that came to her often in the night when her thoughts returned with agonizing precision to the body that went with the man.

But life went on. April saw more snow, as she'd expected. It also saw continued prosperity for *Sweet Serenity*. It saw Serena at her gourmet cooking class every Tuesday night and at the racquetball club with Cynthia every Thursday night. It saw her out on the weekends with Gregory Wolff, a lawyer she dated occasionally, and with Rodney Hendricks, a psychology professor from the university. Both men knew better than to expect commitment from Serena; with each, she kept her private world off limits. Only Tom had penetrated that world—and there was neither sight nor sound of him.

The bouquet he'd sent had long since died, its small basket now a poignant fixture on her dresser, holding the decorative combs and hairclips she wore for the occasional added touch of sophistication. It was an exquisite tortoiseshell fan of a comb that she fished out to wear on the evening of André's party. Pulling her curls straight back into a severe knot, she replayed in her mind the discussion she'd had with André just two days before.

"I don't know," she had hedged. "You know how I hate parties, André."

"But this is *my* party, Serena." His voice had been firm over the phone. "It won't be anything all that big—just a few of my friends. You already know some of them. And there will be several aldermen here. Since you're so bullish on Minneapolis you'll love talking with them."

"I'm sure it will be lovely, André, but I really think I ought to pass it up."

He'd been persistent. "Nonsense. I haven't seen you since I returned from the coast. The party will be quiet and interesting. I'll pick you up myself—say about eight?"

Serena took a stab at an alternative. "Listen, I have an even better idea. I've been taking this gourmet cooking course. Why don't you come over and let me practice the art on you one evening after work next week?"

"Uh-uh, you can't get out of this one so easily. In the first place, between that course and your racquetball and the other gents who follow you around, not to mention my own schedule, we'd never be able to agree on a night. In the second place, an evening alone with you might be more than my wounded heart can take—"

"André," she chided, "so melodramatic . . ."

"Could it be," he struck a hopeful, though teasing note, "that you've changed your mind about *us?* Has absence made the heart grow fonder?"

She sighed at his resort to cliché, smiling patiently. "No, André."

"Then humor me and come to my party," he pressed. "As a friend? Please?"

Serena had had no choice. She didn't want to hurt André; she was, after all, fond of him. And then there was the matter of *Sweet Serenity.* She'd been hesitant about raising the issue of expansion again. If she yielded on the party André might be more approachable.

It was nonetheless with mixed feelings that she found herself dressed in a green silk tunic and pants, with high-heeled gold sandals on her feet, a ghost of lavender

81

on her lids, a touch of mascara on her lashes and a blush of pink on her cheeks. Small pearl buttons graced her ears, a delicate drop to match lay softly on her throat. She was the image of sophistication, with only the shadow of her freckles to betray the lighter spirit within.

The buzzer rang promptly at eight. Within minutes she was downstairs in the lobby greeting her host, sliding into his car, being driven to his spacious home in Kenwood, a section outside downtown Minneapolis. The house was a legacy of the last of his marriage, his ex-wife having happily deserted him to return to New York.

As Serena had often noticed, André's lifestyle was one of lavish consumption. With three ex-wives and a mansion to support, not to mention natty clothes, a late-model sports car and the traveling style of a jet-setter, his financial obligations must have been staggering. Since he never spoke of hardship, she assumed that his work supported him well. *Very well,* she amended the judgment, admiring the artful landscaping, well-lit by floodlights, that surrounded the circular drive leading to his door. *Astoundingly well,* she modified it further, surrendering her light wrap to the uniformed man on duty at the door, taking a glass of champagne from the tray borne by another, and sampling the array of hors d'oeuvres offered to her by a third.

André beamed by her side as he motioned that he wanted to introduce her to several guests whose arrival had preceded theirs. Serena held him back for a minute, putting her hand gently on the sleeve of his black evening jacket.

"I thought you said this was a *small* party," she accused him in a chiding whisper. "You've got at least four or five people in to help here."

André shrugged, smiling without guilt at the deception. "It's really nothing, Serena. Don't worry about it. Clients. Friends. Politicians. Relax, you'll have a good time. Oh, there's Ted Franck from the brokerage firm. Come on, he's anxious to meet you."

Uncomfortably aware that, having arrived on André's arm, she would be considered "with" him, Serena acquiesced for the moment, graciously crossing the room beside him, being her most poised and charming self through the introductions and subsequent conversation. In actuality, it wasn't as bad as she had anticipated. As the guests arrived and the room grew more crowded there was less and less of an opportunity for intimate discussion with anyone. And *that* pleased Serena no end. She strove to keep a low profile, which was why she generally avoided parties. Constantly shuttling from one cluster to the next, she avoided any involvment to speak of—until a firm hand took her elbow just after André had excused himself to attend to business and guided her toward a corner of the large living room.

"How are you, Serena?"

Her head snapped around in instant recognition of the voice. Stunned, she could only stare for several seconds. When she finally spoke she was shakier than she had been all evening. "Tom! What are you doing here?"

"The same thing you are, no doubt." He grinned, spreading a quick fire through her.

"I'm simply obliging André," she went out of her way to explain. "He begged me to come. It seemed to mean so much to him. Now I find that not only are there at least a hundred people here—when he promised me something quiet—but he's disappeared to talk politics with the men." She frowned, still unable to assimilate Tom's presence. "What's *your* excuse? I didn't know that you and André knew each other."

"We don't." Tom looked uneasily around the room. "I was brought by a mutual friend of ours—in fact, I believe he's closeted with her right now."

Serena shook her head. "Uh-uh. He's discussing some

earth-shaking matter with the aldermen. There are several here tonight."

His dark head lowered as he stifled a smile. "He didn't tell you then, the sly fox. Your friend André is with the aldermen, all right. One of them, though, is a *she*."

"Ahh."

"You're not angry?"

"At losing André? Not in the least. He's a friend, nothing more." Her lips thinned in mock chagrin. "But I *am* slightly annoyed at having to put up with this"—she gestured widely toward the crowd milling about the room—"all night."

"Come on." His hand was gentle at the back of her waist. "Let's find a quieter spot."

Had it not been for her irritation at being misled by André, Serena might have thought twice about going anywhere with Tom. After all, the last time she had seen him had been at the racquetball club over a month ago, when they had exchanged nothing more than potent stares. And since then they had exchanged absolutely nothing. Going back a step further, she clearly recalled the morning she had all but thrown herself at him in her apartment. What must he think of her? Then, of course, there was the past. . . .

After ushering her into a small den Tom pulled two easy chairs around to face each other. Serena sank willingly into one, slipping out of her shoes impulsively and curling her legs up under her.

"Comfortable?" he mocked with a smile.

She blushed, aware that her pose wasn't at all in keeping with her sophisticated appearance. "Uh-huh. Finally. My shoes were killing me."

"Famous last words." His eyes caught hers and held them with an intensity that rendered talk superfluous. It seemed forever that they looked at one another, lost in memories, neither wishing to break the spell. To Serena's surprise her thoughts were all positive. Once again she had banished Tom's treachery from mind, aware only of the strength she found so appealing.

"You aren't terribly surprised to find me here," she observed when curiosity finally propelled her on.

Tom smiled in understanding. "I had this funny feeling when Ann mentioned André's name that he was your friend. I don't suppose there are too many investment counselors named André in this area."

"No," she answered softly, admiring the dashing appearance Tom made in his dark European-cut suit. André might have worn the same cut, but it was Tom who carried if off with style, holding himself with just the right air to express self-confidence, rather than arrogance.

"Are you his date?"

Serena grimaced. "He picked me up and brought me here. But I'm certainly not his 'date,' at least not in *my* mind. Anyway, look where his attentiveness has left me—uh, excuse me, that sounded all wrong." Her cheeks burned. "I meant he deserted me quickly enough, and he's really more interested—"

"I know what you mean, Serena. Believe me, I'm not at all offended. Actually, this couldn't have worked out better," he declared smugly.

Not knowing what to say, Serena looked down awkwardly. The rebuff Tom had dealt her that last morning in her apartment was fresh enough to add to her confusion. Even the recollection of the flowers he had sent was small solace for that embarrassment.

"You look beautiful tonight," he began. The gentleness of his voice added to her consternation. "Green becomes you. It picks up the color of your eyes."

"They're hazel." She shrugged. "Nothing spectacular."

"Oh, they're spectacular enough when they get going. Those sparks were the first thing I noticed about you."

The feeling was mutual, but she chose not to enlighten him on that score. Instead she frowned, concentrating on the soft folds of her tunic across her thighs. "You have a knack of inspiring that type of thing."

"Do I still upset you as much?"

"No," she answered half-honestly. "It was the initial shock of seeing you and the memories it dredged up that were so bad. At least I've gotten over the shock." She was certainly not about to mention the new wave of feelings he'd created, many of which were as disturbing in their way as the old, painful memories.

Tom leaned forward to rest his elbows on his knees. He studied her self-consciousness, looked down at his own hands, then spoke his thoughts aloud. "You're a puzzle to me, Serena." That, too, was a mutual sentiment. "On the one hand, you are what you do. You couldn't have chosen a better name. *Sweet Serenity.* It's you." Unsure, she looked up, to be met by a beckoning warmth. "You *are* sweet—I saw you in action in your shop. You genuinely want to please, and you do. Those customers obviously love you as much as your candy. I honestly don't think you'd hurt a soul, unless you were pushed to an absolute extreme."

"I enjoy pleasing people. Perhaps that's why I enjoy *Sweet Serenity* the way I do. But what is it that puzzles you?" she asked.

He amended his choice of word. "Perhaps 'puzzle' is the wrong word. 'Intrigue' may be better." At her baffled look he explained. "It's the part about serenity that's only half true. At the shop, in public places—like that restaurant, this party—you *are* serene. Perhaps it's that you're always serene on the surface—smooth, calm, even—"

"How can you say that, Tom?" she interrupted. *"You've* seen me in a fury. *You've* seen me at my worst. That night, the next morning . . ." Moaning, she looked away. "I'm not particularly proud of the way I acted."

"Don't hold *that* against yourself. We all have our bad

moments. And yours wasn't even all that bad, compared to some."

If he was trying to tell her something she was too enveloped in remorse to hear. "To *me* it was terrible! I've never thrown myself at a man before."

"It wasn't one-sided, Serena," he chided. Again, she barely heard.

"It was horrible! I don't *do* that!"

His whispered "I know" was strangely soothing. She let the silent magic work away some of her tension, aware of the hum of talk from the other room, the strong presence of Tom leaning close to her. When he took her hand in his she didn't pull away. His grip was filled with a reassurance she needed.

"You've made my point beautifully, Serena. You're a very controlled woman, very calm and, yes, serene. But you keep everything bottled up inside. My appearance shocked you enough to punch a tiny hole in that veneer, but I also stirred up enough anger in you to give you a whopper of a headache." He paused, his thumb passing across the back of her hand. "Have you had another since?"

"I haven't seen *you* since," she quipped in retaliation.

His answering look held a determination she hadn't expected. "Well, you *will* be seeing me and I won't have you getting constant migraines. I guess I'll have to teach you to scream and yell rather than lock that tension inside when we're together."

"You must be my self-appointed analyst." Still awkward, she put a hand up out of habit to smooth back her hair.

"You look fine." He caught her at it. "By the way, you looked pretty good on the court."

"So did you. Is that how *you* let off steam? You were playing pretty hard."

"When I wasn't distracted."

"Sorry about that." She smiled shyly. "We didn't

mean to stand there staring but, well, I didn't expect to see you there and then Willie explained that you're a pro, and we amateurs can always use a few pointers."

The light in his eyes was suddenly hotter. "For you, Serena, any time."

Serena stifled the gasp his innate sensuality evoked. Her eyes were bright, held tightly by his. As always, he had that power; now he used it to its fullest. She wanted to protest, but no sound came out. Her mind cried out against the time, the place, the man, but her body stirred toward him as he reached to touch her face.

"I missed you," he whispered, tracing a path of heat from one to the other of her features. "I wanted to call."

"Why didn't you?" she startled herself by asking.

"I didn't want to hurt you. I still don't."

Her own voice was no more than a raw murmur. "Then, why are you here, doing this to me?"

"I'm only touching your face. That's all. It's so smooth and soft and open. . . ."

"Oh, Tom," she cried in soft desperation, "you do so much more to me. Can't you see that?"

He gazed at her with something akin to pain in the depths of his eyes. "Let me kiss you."

"No, don't. . . ."

His head moved closer—or was hers moving to meet it in denial of her protest? "Just once, Serena." His husky murmur warmed her lips, teasing them open with a tenderness that spread excitement through her body. She wanted to resist, but her need of him was greater. Her sensual sigh told him all he wanted to know.

His lips touched hers lightly, caressing them gently, responding to her with controlled fervor. As though fearful of frightening her off, he held the reins of emotion tightly, savoring the sweet opening she offered. He kissed her, then pulled back. Then kissed her again, and pulled back again. Far from using each withdrawal to muster her protests, Serena found herself craving more.

"You taste so good, Serena," he moaned, shifting lithely to perch on the arm of her chair.

She tipped her head back as his lips descended again, welcoming his kiss with the warmth of her mouth and the reciprocal play of her tongue against his. She felt pleasure at the depths she offered him and took pleasure in the feel of his thorough exploration. His fingers splayed across her neck, inching their way toward her throat. Driven by the rippling excitement surging wildly through her, she arched closer. Tom sensed her rising desire and trembled under the strain of restraint. His thumb propped her chin up; his fingertips inched down beneath the silk of her collar, pointing heatedly toward her breast yet unable to move further.

"Let's get out of here," he rasped hoarsely, tearing his lips away to breathe heavily against her temple.

"I can't leave," she gasped, unaware that she clutched his wrist tightly. "André will be looking for me—"

"To hell with André!"

"Tom, he brought me here."

"And I brought Ann. But the two of them are busy enough discussing something. . . ." His words trailed into unexpected silence, arousing Serena's curiosity.

She leaned back in the chair and let her hand fall to her lap. "Who is Ann, anyway?"

"No one important." Gradually his breathing grew steadier.

"She's an alderwoman. She *has* to be someone."

"Not to me."

"You brought her," she pointed out softly.

Tom was momentarily distracted, straightening, standing, walking slowly to the window. His reflection showed a scowl, but when he turned he was under control. "She's an acquaintance. She needed an escort."

Moving quickly, Tom leaned over Serena, his arms on either arm of her chair. "Come on, honey. Let's go somewhere."

"No, I can't."

"To talk?"

"Tom, I can't hurt André like that."

He threw up his hands in frustration. "Sweet Serena! What did I tell you? Always thinking of others. Well, what about *me?*"

The two stared at each other silently, then, with a sigh, Tom lifted a hand to massage his neck, thrust the other in his pants pocket for safekeeping, glared darkly, then stalked from the den to become lost in the crowd.

Serena sat without moving, recalling his final words. "What about *me?*" he had asked, as if he were a child who feared he'd been cheated of some treasure. Was this merely the privileged aristocrat pouting at being thwarted, or was it possible that she'd struck a very private and raw note in Tom? There had been nothing put on about his plea; it had seemed to come from the heart. What should she make of it?

"There you are, Serena. I've been looking all over for you." André advanced with a sure step, his conference evidently finished and matters settled to his satisfaction. "Come on out. There's someone I want you to meet."

She felt no surprise when he led her to a group dominated by a petite, dark-haired firebrand of a woman. Mercifully, Tom was nowhere in sight. "André"—the woman turned at their approach—"this has to be Serena." A cool hand was perfunctorily extended. Serena met it with a matching sense of duty, no more, as André completed the introduction.

"Serena Strickland . . . Ann Carruthers. Ann is one of our esteemed alderpersons, Serena. We're in fine company tonight."

Considering the fact that her mind was on a missing person, Serena managed a cordial exchange that gave proof once more to Tom's insightful analysis. She was sweet and serene, all the while troubled within by the question he had posed. But there were other questions, too, and they nagged at her mercilessly. Where was he now? What was it he wanted? And why did it all matter so much to her, anyway?

It was a definite relief when, after several moments of small talk, Ann was approached and whisked off by another of the guests. Unfortunately, though, André hung on to Serena to guide her through the ever-revolving sea of faces whose names flew past her within seconds of their introduction. Neither Serena's mind nor her heart were on the party.

By pure accident André singled out Tom for attention. "Excuse me," he spoke more formally than usual and with an edge Serena couldn't quite identify. "I don't believe we've met. I'm André Phillips."

To Serena's dismay Tom straightened from the doorjamb against which he'd been leaning, shifted his drink, and met André's outstretched hand. "Tom Reynolds here."

André hesitated for one awkward moment. "Tom Reynolds of the *Bulletin?*"

"The same."

"Then I'm certainly pleased to meet you. Ann did say something about dragging you here." What was intended as humor missed its mark, but neither man seemed to notice.

Serena stood suffering quietly beside André, her eyes glued to Tom's face. She felt the wariness that verged on hostility between the two men and couldn't begin to understand it. André had been the perfect host all evening and Serena knew how adept he was at hiding his feelings, yet here was a dagger nearly unsheathed. Was André interested in Ann? Was *Tom?* As though hearing her silent mention of his name Tom's gaze slid to her face, softening instantly and setting a wholly new set of vibrations astir in the air.

91

André reacted quickly, again out of habit. "I'm sorry. Serena Strickland . . . Tom Reynolds." He paused, studying each in turn. "But you two know each other, don't you?" he asked, fitting the first piece into the puzzle. He clearly recalled the incident at the restaurant over a month ago. Then Serena had denied knowing Tom; now the expression on her face made a mockery of that denial.

It was Tom who came to Serena's aid, a knight in shining armor. "We met earlier," he answered noncommittally, avoiding a direct lie, but very clearly protecting her secret. Serena's eyes transmitted their thanks as she nodded in ostensible greeting.

André, however, was less concerned with the connection than he was in gleaning information. "I understand you've begun to make some changes at the *Bulletin*."

"A few." Tom kept his distance. "I've only been there a very short time. I'll need a while longer to have any kind of impact."

André's smile lacked its usual perfection. "So you are planning to stir things up? I'd heard rumors to that extent."

"I'm planning to turn the *Bulletin* into a first-rate newspaper. If that takes stirring up, as you put it, then I'll be stirring things up."

"It must be a difficult business," André went on pointedly. "There seems to be a backlash against newspapers and the power they wield." Serena stiffened at his latent hostility, but neither man noticed. "I read about more and more law suits, for libel. You folks have to be very careful."

While Serena's stomach twisted at the direction the conversation was taking Tom seemed utterly calm. "We always have been and still are. That's not to say that the occasional irresponsible reporter can't do some damage. But it's up to the editorial staff to prevent wanton mudslinging." He tipped his head in a self-assured manner. "I'm not worried about the *Bulletin*. We'll have our facts straight."

"Excuse me," Serena broke in, unable to bear the discussion any longer. "I'm going to freshen up." She spoke softly to André, nodding to Tom as she turned and walked with forced steadiness through the crowd, into the foyer, down the hall, and into the peace of the bathroom. When she emerged her direction was even more sure. Retracing her steps, she stood at the entrance to the living room, located the tall figure she wanted and approached him without hesitation.

"Could we leave, Tom?" she whispered, not fully understanding her action, only knowing that she wanted to go . . . with Tom.

"André?"

"I'll leave a message with . . . the butler." She smirked, then sobered in a silent plea, slipping her hand into Tom's, seeking his strength. His fingers tightened as he drew her beside him. She began to breathe freely only once she'd been comfortably settled in the front seat of his two-seater Mercedes. Leaning her head back, she closed her eyes and listened to the sounds as he slid behind the wheel, turned the key in the ignition, shifted into gear, and accelerated, leaving behind the bright-lit mansion and its crowd of party-goers, including, she thought quite happily, André. He had offended her with his subtle attack on Tom, though he had done nothing more than express sentiments with which she agreed wholeheartedly. Had she grown that protective of Tom that she took *his* side on such an issue? Impossible! She was simply tired.

Eyes still shut, she felt the gentle touch of Tom's fingers on her cheek. "Headache?" he asked softly.

"No. I'd just had enough."

The steady hum of the well-tuned engine was soothing. Serena felt strangely calm and totally trusting of her driver.

"Not a party girl?"

She chuckled. "Not by a long shot." Then she quickly opened her eyes. "Oh, Tom, if you wanted to stay—"

"No, no." He held out a hand to stop her. "I prefer my evenings quieter. I only went at Ann's urging, but she really didn't need an escort. I'm sure she won't miss me."

"Will she be expecting you to take her home?"

His smile was barely visible in the darkness. "I left *my* message with the butler, too. It's good to know he's served some practical purpose for the money he's being paid."

"Do you like Ann?"

"Sure I like her. But if I wanted to be with her I wouldn't be driving you home right now."

For the first time Serena glanced out the front windshield. "Tom, you're going in the wrong direction. We have to head back toward the city to get to my apartment."

"We're not going there."

"But you said—"

"Home. *My* home."

With the tension of the party gone a new wave of emotion swept over her. "Oh, Tom. I don't know." She remembered his kiss, her kiss, earlier that evening. "I think you should turn around."

"No way."

"Tom . . ."

But he had no intention of altering course, despite her soft plea. Rather, he grew more adamant. "We're going to my place to talk, Serena. There's an awful lot I want to say, and even more I want to hear."

"Tom, I don't know if I'm up to this."

"You've had a month!" With the force of his exclamation he swerved to the side of the road and stepped firmly on the brakes, his arm shooting out to hold her in place. When the car had come to a complete stop he turned to

her, leaving only the memory of his strength where his
arm had been a moment before.

"Listen, Serena. There's something we have to hash
out. Until we do we'll both be in limbo."

"No."

"Yes! Don't try to deny your response to me. I felt it
back in that den tonight. I felt it back in your apartment
that morning. Damn it, I felt it in that restaurant that very
first day!"

"You're confusing the issue, Tom," she argued softly.
"That first day I was stunned to see you—"

"Could it be that there was something more, even
then? It happens sometimes, you know. Instant response.
Biological attraction. Chemical communication."

"No."

"You're *that* sure?" Darkness hid his expression, but
his profile was uncompromising.

Serena shivered as she stared at him, simultaneously
trying to consider and dismiss his claim. In the end she
had to be honest, with him and with herself. "No," she
admitted wretchedly.

Tom started the engine. "Then let's go. We'll work this
all out, one way or the other. I've got to know what's
going on in that head of yours or I'm apt to go right off
the deep end myself."

"Hmph . . . true justice . . ."

He ignored her sally. "Justice is your giving me an
hour of your time in return for my rescuing you from
André's party."

Serena's eyes glittered in the passing headlights.
"From the frying pan into the fire?" she quipped dryly,
quietly, but not quietly enough.

"There's always been a fire with us, Serena. That's
what this is all about. Fire can be either destructive or
purifying. Either we douse it for good, or we let it flame."

His point was well-taken, expressing much of Serena's

own sentiment. Tom had been on her mind enough in the past month to merit this time spent together. He was right; it *had* to be. For her own peace of mind as much as for his, they had to talk things out. Talk was good for the soul. But the body, what would answer its needs?

"I'll take you home later, if that's what you want." Tom spoke gently, reading her mind, in total understanding of her fear. It was this very understanding that reassured her, and the fact that she did trust him. "OK?" he asked.

She hesitated for just a moment before giving the only answer conscience would allow. "OK," she murmured and he purposefully stepped on the gas.

5

For a Saturday night the traffic was negligible, reducing what might have been a drive of forty minutes to a simple twenty-minute trip.

"I didn't realize that you lived in Wayzata," Serena commented, easily recognizing her surroundings.

Tom's eyes remained fixed on the road. "There's a lot about me you don't know. Which will be changed soon enough."

She shot him a slanted look. "Why does that sound ominous?"

"Does it?" he asked innocently. "I hadn't meant it to be ominous. Perhaps . . . enticing?"

"Oh, yes, enticing." Her echo held enough amusement to cover the trepidation she felt. What had she let herself in for?

"Having second thoughts?"

"Naturally."

"I wouldn't do anything to hurt you. You know that, don't you?"

97

Serena answered impulsively. "I wish you had made that promise years ago. My family might still be in one piece."

"No, Serena. If it hadn't been me it would have been someone else—reporter, detective, district attorney, take your pick. Your father broke the law. He had no one to blame but himself."

"You didn't know him," she argued softly, lowering her gaze while images of her childhood passed before her. "He was a good man. . . ."

Tom considered her words and, more important, the heartfelt belief behind them. Serena had adored her father; even now, though she might acknowledge that he'd done wrong, she could not think of him as a criminal. In her dreams she often imagined him vindicated through the process of appeal. In reality he hadn't lived long enough.

"Here we are." With a turn of the wheel Tom turned from the main road onto a private drive that wound around for a short distance and ended in a graceful arc.

"Tom, this is beautiful!" Serena exclaimed, captivated at once by the moonlit manor before her. In the total absence of artificial light its profile was impressive—tall in the eaves, broad in the wings, and strong in the sturdy brick of which it was molded. "It's you!"

Scrambling from the car, she was aware of Tom's instant materialization by her side. "It will be one day. Come on"—he took her hand—"we go over this way."

Bemused, she followed his lead, away from the larger house toward a small cottage on its far side. She heard the gentle sounds of her high heels tapping on the flagstone walk, the wind playing through branches just shy of their spring buds, and a softer, more rhythmic lilt from the lake nearby. But the hand of night was reluctant to reveal more than one bit of beauty at a time. Serena clutched Tom's long fingers as he headed toward the single lighted lamppost.

"Tom?"

"Uh-huh?" He fished in his pocket for a key.

"I'm not sure I understand."

"What?" Amusement lacing his tone, he opened the door, reached within to switch on a light, and stood to the side for Serena to pass.

"The house . . . *that* house, is *it* yours or is *this?*"

"Would it matter?" he drawled tartly.

She shrugged. "Only to satisfy my curiosity, or if I needed an address to send a quart-sized carton of Cinnamon Red Hots to."

"You'd be that cruel?"

"You wouldn't *have* to eat them," she said sweetly over her shoulder as she stepped across the threshold of the quaint brick structure and found herself in a surprisingly open single room, contemporary both in design and furnishing. "This is amazing, Tom! This is like a modern mountain hideaway."

The soft click of the door as it closed added to the intimacy of the surroundings. As she admired the long, plush-cushioned velour sofa and matching armchairs, the low coffee table, the free-standing television and stereo unit with its sectioned desk and inevitable typewriter, she felt a surge of warmth.

"You like it?" he asked.

Her hazel eyes sparkled her approval. "It's delightful. Do you really live here, rather than at that house?"

"For now."

"And what does that mean?"

"It means," he sighed, "that I can't be bothered by the worries of running a large house. This is just my size."

Surprised, Serena turned to stare at him. "You do own the house?"

His firm lips rose at the corners. "I had to buy it to get this."

"Tom"—she frowned through a skeptical smile—

"that's ludicrous. People don't buy huge estates simply to live in small cabins."

"You may have a point," he rejoined tongue in cheek. "To be more precise, what I really wanted was a small place on the lake. I had to buy the whole parcel of land, with the woods surrounding it, to get the privacy I wanted. The house was thrown in as a bonus."

Serena chuckled. "Some bonus!" But she grew more serious. "You really do want privacy?"

"Yes."

"But why? From what I can imagine, given the fact that your family is a prominent one, you must have been raised in the public eye. I'd think you'd be used to it."

He gestured toward the sofa, watched as she sank into it, then eased his long frame onto its far end. Appreciative of the distance he'd deliberately put between them, Serena relaxed.

"I may be well used to the limelight, but that doesn't mean I have to like it. From the start I preferred a more private life."

"Could've fooled me." She looked away.

"Even then. What you saw of me was my job. There was—there is—a private man behind the notebook."

It was his vehemence that coaxed her eyes back to him. She might have been dubious still, but she wanted to know more. "So you bought this place. You've done it over?" Again she perused the decor, admiring the palette of browns and creams, accessorized in gray to emphasize the masculine tone.

Tom nodded. "Privacy doesn't rule out convenience. I bought the estate when I first arrived here, then lived in a hotel while the interior of the cottage was completely torn out and redone. It needed wiring, plumbing, plastering— everything." Tipping his head back, he smiled. "Not bad, if I do say so myself. I enjoy it here."

"Where do you *live?*" she burst out, qualifying her question at his frown. "I mean, this seems to be the only

100

room. I assume that's the kitchen"—she pointed—"and that's the bath, but . . . ?"

Tom leaned forward, his voice a hair lower. "If you're asking about the sleeping arrangements, you're sitting on them."

"The couch? You don't sleep on the couch every night, do you?"

"Now, now, don't knock what you haven't seen. It just so happens that this couch is no ordinary couch. It opens into the most comfortable king-sized bed you've ever seen."

"That's not saying much, since I haven't seen many." Her quip was as pointed as she dared make it without inspiring Tom to revenge. As it was, she was at a disadvantage, here in this cozy cabin with him. Granted, his tall and muscled frame lounged several feet away, but her pulse fluttered strangely every time she looked at him. And it certainly didn't help to know that they were sitting on his bed. It was like sipping champagne from a loving cup.

As if he had caught her thought Tom unfolded his limbs and rose in one smooth motion. "Would you like some wine?"

Feeling in sudden need of fortification, she nodded. "That would be nice." But her mind was still on the king-sized bed. "Tell me, Tom. Once before you said you'd been 'burned.' What did you mean by that?"

"You *are* curious."

"*You* were the one who suggested we talk. And *you* were the one who pointed out how little I know about you."

Tom remained silent for a time, bent in concentration over a conveniently stubborn cork. With its climactic pop he seemed to reach a decision.

"I was married once. It was a long time ago. I was—we both were—very young." Returning to the sofa, he handed her an empty glass, skillfully filled it halfway, then retreated to his end of the couch to fill his own glass and sink back in a posture of brooding. "She had an image in her mind of what she wanted from life, with riches and glamour ranking high on her list. I guess I was a disappointment."

"A disappointment?" she asked, incredulous. "How can that be? Certainly you could have given her all that."

"To Eleanor, wealth was a goal in itself. To me, it's simply the means to an end that may be totally different, such as the modesty of this cabin. I realize that to you my attitude may sound callllous. In my life money has never been a problem and most likely never will. In that respect I *am* arrogant, I suppose." His brow furrowed beneath the swath of dark hair that the evening breeze had ruffled. "I enjoy the finer things in life, but in a very private, very personal way."

There was something comforting in what he said, for Serena was, herself, a private soul. "But your wife couldn't agree?"

"Hah! She couldn't *stand* it. I put up with the parties and the globe-trotting as much as I could, but there's a limit for every man beyond which he simply can't go. When it became clear that we were headed in different directions in life we called it quits."

"A mutual decision?" Serena asked softly, touched by his willingness to share this intimacy, sensing that he rarely did so.

At last he looked at her. "Yes. Fortunately there were no children. It was difficult enough."

"You loved her."

"Yes." He took a deep breath. "In my way I did love her."

"Do you ever see her?"

He shook his head and studied the smooth swirl of wine as he moved his glass. "She's married again. He's a European hotelier. From what I hear they have several kids already."

Serena was aware of the vulnerability in him, of the hurt he must have suffered. Much as she wanted to attribute only the harshest qualities to him she couldn't ignore the more human element that never failed to touch her deeply.

"Do you want them? Kids?" she prodded gently.

"Sure." He smiled impulsively, then again more sadly. "That's what the big house is for. Someday . . . perhaps . . ."

Serena ached with the dying off of his voice. She actually wanted to slide across the distance and hold him, comfort him, even promise him those things he wished. *It was absurd!* This was Thomas Harrison Reynolds! How could she sympathize with *him?*

"That's a strange expression you're wearing," Tom observed, suddenly more humorous, as though freed of a burden. "It's a combination of compassion and anger." He paused. "What are you thinking, Serena?"

"I'm thinking that you totally confuse me. You're not at all what I expected to find."

Tom stared at her in silence. His features grew more gentle with each passing second. When he finally spoke it was very softly. "That has to be a compliment. I can imagine what it took for you to offer it."

She burst from the couch, nearly spilling her wine, and paced to the low-silled window on the far side of the room. "It's the truth. Unfortunately."

"Unfortunately?"

Her hazel-eyed gaze locked with his as she turned. "It would have been so much easier to hate you. With everything that happened back in L.A., I *should* hate you!"

He rose from the sofa with an animal grace that evoked a similarly primitive response in Serena. "But you don't," he stated quietly. Again she was perplexed, for where there might have been triumph on his face there was only a look of gratitude.

"No," she whispered, mesmerized once more by the manly strength of his features, now hovering dangerously close.

"Do you hate yourself for that?"

"I don't know. I can't think when you're around."

"Oh, Serena," he murmured, kissing her with the same gentleness that puzzled her so. Responding to the longing within she returned the kiss in kind, expressing that irrational desire to protect and comfort through the warmth of her lips as they moved against his. But there was still so much to be said, and Serena was not up for rejection just yet. It was she who broke the tender embrace.

"Tom, we have to talk. You said so yourself." The words ran into each other with the speed of her racing heart. "This is the problem. It's so easy to become lost in . . . in . . ."

"Desire?"

She looked down, nervously fingering a button of his shirt, barely aware of her action. "Yes. Desire."

"It's a beautiful thing, isn't it?"

The warmth of his body reached out to her fingertips, counteracting her desperate attempt at self-control. A frown tugged at her brows, marring the face he had earlier called serene.

"I'm—I'm not sure."

"Now, what's *that* supposed to mean?" He closed his large palms around her shoulders but held her at arm's reach, demanding an explanation.

"Just that," she insisted unhappily. "I'm not sure."

"Come on, Serena. You've been honest so far. Don't stop now. It's one of the things I admire about you. Why can't you admit to the pleasure you feel in my arms?"

Embarrassed, she tried to pull away, but his grip tightened. "I *do* admit to that pleasure. But desire, and its end . . ." She looked down again. "It's been a very long time. . . ."

"Ahh," he crooned, drawing her against the solid wall of his chest and cradling her there. "So you *are* thinking of the future. That's a good sign."

"I don't know about that either," she moaned, fighting the havoc wreaked by the mingling scent of wine and man that permeated her senses and clouded her brain. "If anything I feel more guilty thinking about it now than I did then."

Tom grew still, let his chin fall to the crown of her head for a pensive moment, then released her. "You're right," he sighed. "We have to talk." Again he gestured toward the sofa. Again she sat. This time, however, he stood more warily before her. "OK, Serena, let's have it out. First of all, I'm going to tell you what's on *my* mind." With a brief pause, his gaze grew darker, if possible, even more intense. By intuition alone Serena read his thoughts. But he spoke clearly, boldly.

"I want you, Serena. It's as simple as that. I want you. I want to be with you, to get to know you. Right now I want to take you to bed and make love to you. There! Are you shocked?"

"I'm twenty-nine years old, Tom. Shocked? No. Frightened? Very."

"You've got nothing to fear from me, honey. I've told you as much before."

"It's not *you,* Tom." Her lips thinned in frustration. Sighing, she shook her head in disgust. "It's me. Things may happen between the two of us that I can't control. I'll want them while they're happening, but how do I live with myself afterward?"

Even now, she craved the protective solace of his arms. Yet he stood alone before her, legs planted firmly in a wide stance, hands on his ruggedly narrow hips. "Then we're back to the issue of guilt. And I *know* that the guilt would have little to do with the actual act of making love, would it?"

She shook her head, missing the bouncing shelter of

the hair which usually fell so freely but which was still anchored firmly at the nape of her neck. "We're living in modern times—"

"And you've lived the life of a nun for the past ten years."

"What is this, Tom? Would you rather I slept my way through life, consorting with every man who crossed my path? It just so happens that *that* doesn't appeal to me!" Scowling, she burrowed deeper into the cushions. "Sex has to mean something. It's not something I'd do for desire alone."

"You thought you loved this—what was his name—Lowry?"

"I did, at the time."

"And do you love me?"

"Love has nothing to do with this."

"But you'd go to bed with me."

"No!" She jumped up, then stormed out of his reach. "I haven't said that either."

"You implied it."

"You twist everything I say!"

"But you want me?"

"I want you out of my life!"

"Let's try desire. You desire me?"

She whirled around, eyes flashing with anger. "Damn it, yes! I desire you—if we're down to playing word games. I'm human. I have natural cravings. I'm a woman! And yes, I *desire* you!" She spat out the word with scorn.

"You've made your point." He sighed in defeat, astonishing her with his blunt capitulation. She watched warily as he retrieved his wineglass, filled it again, and strode to the window to stare into the night.

Serena was more confused than ever. She'd told him the things he wanted to hear, yet he seemed more lost than before. Drawn by the same enigmatic force that confounded her, she found herself approaching the window, putting her hand on his arm.

"I'm sorry. That sounded so angry."

"You *are* angry, honey. That's the point." He glanced sidelong down at her.

"The point," she confessed, "is that when you look at me like that and call me 'honey' the anger I feel vanishes. It's *that* that terrifies me."

Tom turned slowly, cradling her face in his rough palms. "What if I said that I was just as frightened? Would you believe me?"

"You? Frightened?"

"Yes."

"Of what?"

"Involvement." His gaze traced electrifying circles around her face.

"With me?" With the strength of a reflex built up over years she stiffened. "Because of me? My family?"

"No! No! Serena, how can you say something like that?"

Her eyes glistened. "It happened once before, Tom. I can't forget it."

"I know," he whispered, caressing her cheeks with his thumbs. "I know." The tenderness of his tone sent shivers of arousal through her body. He was close and warm and understanding of her every emotion. "Oh, Serena," he gasped. "It's happening again. It's the same with me, Serena, something I can't seem to control." His lips lowered to brush against her forehead in agony. "I want you so."

Serena felt the tremor that shook him shudder through her own limbs. She closed her eyes as sanity receded, then opened them quickly to grasp common sense.

"We can't, Tom," she moaned softly. "This is wrong. It's not good for either of us." But her hands itched to touch him and she did, reaching out to circle his waist with her arms and move against his manhood with a tormented sigh. "Oh, Tom . . ." Her words echoed in the far depths of his mouth, his lips seizing hers with the same fierceness that inflamed her entire body. What had begun at the party that night—what had begun a month ago in the restaurant—seemed destined for completion. Serena wanted Tom more than anything she could have imagined. Her body ached for his vibrant pulse, for the possession that would bring her to fruition as a woman, complete and loved if only for the evening.

"What if we were to pretend," Tom began, breathing raggedly by her ear, "that we had no past? That we were two different people? That we were in love?"

Serena put her arms up over his sinewy shoulders and clung tightly, burying her face against the warm, beating pulse in his neck. "We're adults, Tom," she whispered, tasting the heady tang of him as she acted the devil's advocate. "We can't play games."

He stroked her back, pressing her closer as his fingers drew erotic designs on the clinging silk of her tunic top. "We have to do *something*. I've tried staying away for a month, a whole month, and look where it's left me. I feel more out of control than ever." His teeth settled on the lobe of her ear, nipping it, grating against the gleaming pearl of her earring. "You look beautiful tonight. I could have taken you there in that den of André's."

Serena measured the strength of his back with her palms splayed over its muscular breadth. "Oh, Tom," she sighed wistfully. "Why did you ever show up there tonight?"

His fine shiver of tension passed easily as an extension of passion. "Let's call it fate, Serena," he murmured, crushing her more fiercely to his taut frame. "It's the same thing that brought us eye to eye in the restaurant that first day."

"But I would never have stared if I hadn't recognized you." Even as she offered the feeble protest she knew it to be a dubious point. Tom himself had planted the seeds of doubt in her mind. Would she have sought him out regardless? Was there indeed an unfathomable attraction surpassing all else that brought them together?

"We'll never know for sure," he argued softly. "What if . . . what if we'd never seen each other before that day? Would you be wanting me now?"

"Yes. Oh, yes." Her body rippled with swelling excitement at the seductive timbre of his voice. Her hands found their way to his waist, granting eager fingers the free exploration of his firm, hard body. She could only repeat his name, over and over again, as though hypnotized.

"Pretend?" he begged with an urgency that thrilled her as much as the iron-strong hands that worked their way almost timidly across her body to the side bow that held her tunic wrapped about her waist. A single tug released it and Serena knew she had reached the moment of decision. Even amid the thick sensual fog settling heavily over them she could still see her way clear to escape, if she wanted to.

"Serena, what *do* you want?" Without doubt he wavered at his own point of no return. She could feel it in the thrust of his body.

"Heaven help me, Tom. *I want you!*" she cried in the agony of responding for the sake of raw pleasure. "I'll pretend. I'll pretend. I need you, Tom." The last was without pretense.

His answering groan was an excruciating one. "Oh, Serena. Come here, love."

"I'm here. I'm yours." She gloried in the game, reaching in wonder to touch his face, exploring each manly feature with her fingertips. The depth of his eyes, his brows, the strong line of his nose and lean planes of his cheeks, the faint rasp of the beard that had been shaved hours before, the jaw that spoke of the character she was just beginning to know. With an imperceptible movement of his head he captured a wandering finger and sucked on it deeply. "Tom!" she gasped, quavering his name mindlessly.

"Pretend." He murmured the watchword again, drawing her into the safe harbor of his arms, pressing his lips to hers and parting them easily with the moistened tip of his tongue.

Serena melted like ice from a wintry mountaintop flowing surely to warm lower pastures. When he held her back to slip open her blouse the chill was a momentary thing. His hands, male-textured against the smoothness of her flesh, quickly replaced the discarded fabric, covering her with the searing heat of desire.

"Beautiful Serena," he breathed against her neck when his hands moved upward to cup the gentle fullness of her lace-covered breasts. She arched toward his palms instinctively, feeling the explosive need to be his at once.

But he was the master, prolonging every bit of his heaven and hers, as though they'd never make it there again. Slowly he reached to release the catch of her bra and peeled off the wisp of material to let spill the ivory wealth of her. She was naked from the waist up and at his mercy. His eyes devoured the twin swells before he loosed his questing fingers to her flesh.

"How can you be so cruel?" she whimpered at his tantalizing play, crying out when he took each nipple between thumb and forefinger and rubbed sweet pain round and about them.

"It's all in the game," he gritted back, the pain his own as well.

"Then I'm playing too." Deliberately Serena tugged loose the knot of his tie, released each button of his shirt and pushed the fine fabric from his shoulders to join her silk tunic on the floor. Leaning forward, she put her lips to his chest and kissed her way across its matted plain. The path she left was moist and heady. She thrilled to the success of her revenge, evident in the intermittent groans he gave.

And Serena pretended. On Tom's prescription she pretended that there had never been a scandal sixteen years ago. She pretended that she'd seen Tom that day in the restaurant for the first time in her life, that there was nothing, *nothing* to keep them apart. She offered herself up to the fantasy of womanhood, believing Tom's words as he finished undressing her. "So lovely . . ."

The sofa was their bed, though neither thought to unfold it or seek the sheets that would be inside. The plushness of velour was a regal mattress, the narrowness every bit wide enough for one body atop another.

She lay where he had eased her back, naked, watching as he quickly matched her in that state. Bare-chested, his body had been intimidating in its virile pull. Now, totally nude, it instilled a mindless frenzy that tremored continually through her. She reached for him when he approached, then cried aloud when he came down to her. His flesh was hot against hers, sending a now-familiar fire raging to each of her nerve ends in turn.

Her hands grasped the smoother flesh of his hips and urged him closer. But he was not to be rushed in the illusion of love. His gaze smoldered as he lingered, savoring the touch of his lines on hers. With a leisure that heightened her cravings even more he took her hands, kissing them both, holding them to his lips as he looked with slow thoroughness over her body.

"Tell me again," she pleaded with a shudder at the last shadow of doubt.

"Pretend. Pretend. We're two people with no past. Only each other. Now." He paused. "I love you." Softly: "I love you." With more conviction.

Her heart stopped, then burst with need. "And I love you," she whispered. Again. And again.

Having said the words that made it all possible, the fantasy was nearly complete. A hoarse and primitive sound reverberated from Tom's throat to be muffled against her breasts as he lowered his head. His mouth found the crest it sought, surrounding and sucking the rosy peak, sending an urgent message to the heart of Serena's femininity.

"Don't keep me waiting, Tom," she moaned, writhing beneath him. "I need you. Please . . . now . . ." In an instinctive surge toward ecstasy she arched her hips against the boldness of his. "Now!" she cried a final time before he seized her lips and his body covered her.

His muscled thigh parted her legs and Serena gasped loudly as he filled her both physically and spiritually. She was part of him and he of her; the joy of that knowledge lavished sensual satisfaction through her entire being.

Tom kissed her as he set the pace, slow at first, then with driven speed as he, too, fell victim to the ancient and primal force that brought them together. Serena answered his heat with the fervor of a woman possessed, meeting his passion equally, relinquishing herself totally to the soaring unreality. Her hands measured the strain of his muscles, then lost all awareness when her own senses blinded her to everything but his body—on her, in her.

Together they built, then peaked, then toppled, drenched in each other's sweat, limbs intertwined. Fighting the return to reality Tom stayed inside her, clasping her body to his only until his ardor returned. Then, in a miraculous repeat, they loved once again.

It was a long, long time before Serena's breathing steadied and her quivering body stilled. She lay against Tom, her head on his damp chest, her leg thrown intimately over and between his. Neither said a word for fear of shattering the illusion that had brought such pleasure, such utter fulfillment.

Tom spoke at last, but only after he had brought his free arm around to lock tight the circle in which he held her. "I knew it would be like that, Serena. I knew it from the first." Eyes shut against the cushioning hair of his chest, she savored his words through the lingering haze of her passion. "It's the fire inside you, love. The same fire that pits us against one another has the power to let you love me the way you did." She felt the warmth of his breath as he tucked his chin in to look down at her. "I've never seen such passion, Serena. It's innocent at the same time as it's worldly and wild. How can that be?"

"I don't know." She smiled, shifting more snugly against him. Even the slow return of reality could do nothing to dampen the contentment she felt by his side. "You seem to bring out the basest instincts in me!"

He chuckled. "You can say that again."

"No need," she murmured, brushing her lips against a taut male nipple, then smiling at his response.

"Come here," he growled, surprising her when he pulled her over him and went to work at the back of her neck. "I should have done this earlier. Your hair is too lovely to tie back, even if it *did* look gorgeous tonight." Within seconds he'd freed her auburn tresses and spread them gently over her shoulders. "There," he breathed in deep satisfaction. "That's better." He surveyed his hand-iwork for a moment longer before easing her down beside him again.

"How do you feel?" he asked, pausing. "I didn't hurt you, did I?"

Serena smiled. "That's a dumb question. Did I seem like I was hurting?"

"I'm not sure. At one point there I thought I felt nails digging into my back."

"You're wicked."

"I'm serious." Again he paused, this time quite mean-ingfully. "Are you all right?"

Her soft-whispered "yes" was poignant.

"Are you sorry?"

"No."

"Do you feel guilty?"

"Not now."

"But you will?"

"Probably."

"I won't," he declared. "Not ever. It was beautiful, what we just shared."

"Beautiful, but dangerous." She thought of the future, of the taste of Tom that lingered in her mouth, her veins, her heart. Could one become addicted so easily? Or had she simply chosen to ignore the earlier signs, the thoughts of him during the last month, the memories of his hands and kisses and care?

He cupped her chin and lifted it, forcing her eyes to meet his. "Dangerous as in pregnancy?"

Serena was stunned. "I hadn't even thought of that." When Tom exhaled loudly and shook his head she misinterpreted his gesture. "I'm sorry. Don't worry, I would never hold you respon—"

"Serena!" He squeezed her into silence. "That's not what I meant at all."

"Then what?"

"I just marvel at you. Your purity and honesty. I've never met anyone like you."

"And if I *did* become pregnant? Would you be marveling then?"

"Yes." There was no doubt in his voice.

But Serena's held enough for them both. "You wouldn't mind my bearing your child?"

"Of course not."

"Even knowing what you know?" At his frown she elaborated. "Even knowing that the truth would come out one day?"

Taken off guard, Tom let her go when Serena scrambled over him suddenly. Heading for the bathroom, she stopped short, hung her head, and waited. She knew what it was that had just driven her from Tom's arms, but she wasn't ready for it.

"Don't do this to yourself," he groaned from directly behind, turning her into his arms to rescue her again. "I've told you once that the past doesn't matter to me. If I could do it all over again I'd do things differently. But it's done. I can't change what happened then. And it has no bearing on what's happening now." Cupping her face in the power of his hands, he tilted it up. "Don't you see, when I look at you I see none of the past. I only see now, and tomorrow."

Serena was unprepared for this softness, just as she'd been unprepared for all the very positive things she'd discovered about Tom. She was drawn to him, excited by him beyond belief. The thought of never seeing him after this night was as painful as the thought of living with this ghost from the past. Her eyes brimmed in anguish as she returned the intensity of his gaze with her own.

"Oh, Tom, what am I going to do?"

6

~~~~~~~~~~~~~

Tom kissed her tenderly. "What you're going to do, Serena, is to stand right here for just a minute." He touched her lips lightly with his, then proceeded to convert the sofa into the king-sized bed he'd touted earlier that evening.

Serena watched him as he worked. She tried desperately to be as nonchalant about his nakedness as he appeared to be, yet she found herself entranced, unable to look away. His body was spectacular, that of an athlete, well-toned and muscular, with the coordination to match.

"Do you play tennis, too?" she asked impulsively.

Pausing in his work, Tom straightened and grinned. "How could you tell?"

In answer her eye fell to trace the faded lines of his tan, the faint ring on his upper arms, his calves, his thighs.

"Are you disappointed?" he smiled crookedly, standing boldly still.

"That you play tennis?" She groped for reason, far too aware of her own nudity as she studied his.

"That I'm forty, with the body to prove it."

"Tom, it never *occurred* to me to think of your age." But she grinned. "You must be searching for compliments. You know you're in your prime."

The gleam in his eye teased her further, though he bent to finish his work. "There! Now, *you*, Serene Highness, go here." Leading her lightly by the hand, he sat her in bed. "I'll be your backrest." Climbing agilely in beside her he propped pillows high beneath his head and drew her down against his chest.

"Now what?" she whispered, unsure once more.

"Now we talk."

Serena exploded into giddy laughter. "Talk? You make me feel like a very naked queen and expect me to talk?"

"Would you rather make love again?"

"Shame on you, Tom." She fought fire with fire. "You're forty years old. Are you really up to it again?"

Without warning he slithered over her, trapping her in his web of masculinity. "That will definitely cost you," he growled half-playfully, pinning her hands to either side. "Kiss me."

"We'll talk."

"Kiss me!"

"Tom, this won't solve anything—"

"Kiss me!" The fire in his eyes was the same that she identified so strongly with the cub reporter of her memory.

"Please," she pleaded. "You frighten me when you look at me like that."

He softened instantly but held her still. "I'm sorry, love. It's what you do to me. I could make love to you all night. But we *do* have to talk. Now,"—he grinned—"just a little kiss."

Telling herself that she acted only to please him,

117

Serena raised her lips to his and delivered what she intended to be a "little kiss." Somewhere between "little" and "kiss," though, she found herself partner in a volatile venture that threatened an imminent explosion. He let go of her hands and she used her freedom to start a foray of her own that left him shuddering with reawakening excitement.

"What was that you were saying about my age?"

Through the pleasure of what she felt she couldn't be angry. "I was saying that you are very definitely in your prime. And that we should talk."

"Serena."

"Yes?"

"Uh . . . that's enough . . ."

"Something wrong?"

"Serena!"

"What is it, Tom? Speak up."

"Damn it, Serena. I can't think rationally, let alone talk, unless you stop what you're doing!"

"You started it."

"*You* stop it!"

Feeling eminently powerful, Serena tormented him for a moment longer before leisurely trailing her fingertips up his body to the throbbing pulsepoint at his neck. "Better?" she crooned sweetly.

Her humor eluded Tom. "Give me a minute," he rasped, taking several deep and steadying breaths. Finally he gave an exaggerated sigh. "All right. We talk."

"Tell me about your work."

He opened one lazy eye to look at her. "*I* should talk?"

"Yes."

"What do you want to know?"

"What you do."

He sighed patiently. "I publish newspapers."

"*Every day*, Tom. What do you actually *do?*"

When his answer was slow in coming she looked up at

118

him, resting her chin on his chest. He was studying her closely. "Why are you asking me this, Serena? I would have thought it was just what you wouldn't want to hear. As a matter of fact, I'm amazed at your calmness."

His line of thought was easy to follow. "So am I," she whispered almost to herself, lying back on the sheet and staring at the ceiling. "I'm not quite sure I understand *myself*."

"And that's what *I* want to discuss. You. Your feelings. About what just happened. About what happened sixteen years ago." Tom rolled to his side and propped himself up on an elbow. Serena turned her head sideways to look at him.

"This is all so strange," she began, struggling to piece together the puzzle. "I mean, here I am . . . lying here . . . with you."

"And you seem very complacent about it all. Very serene."

For an instant her hazel gaze flared. "What would you prefer? That I rant and rave? Scream that you made me do it? I'm not that way, Tom. You should know that by now!"

"But, I didn't—"

"*I know that!* That's just the point. Nothing has happened here that I didn't want to happen. I enjoyed every minute of your lovemaking." She was about to mention the game, then thought better of it. What had begun as an illusion had burgeoned into the real thing. The thought hit her with stunning force. Looking away, she fought the abrupt awareness of her emotions. When she turned her head toward him once more there was sadness in her eyes. "It's odd, what's happened. When I'm with you, looking at you, touching you, wanting you to do the same to me, I can't remember who you are. I only *feel* things now. You blot out all thoughts of what I should be remembering." Her voice rose in agitation.

119

"And the worst of it is that, even right now, I'm not sorry. I don't *want* to remember anything. I know it's there, but I can very happily push it out of my mind—at least until tomorrow."

"It *is* tomorrow, love," Tom spoke on a sober note. "And we've got to work this out. You've created a dichotomy in your mind. On the one hand, there's the Tom Reynolds whom you hate on sight. On the other, there's me."

She grimaced. "Very well put."

"The question is, how do we bring the two together?"

For the first time since she'd sought the solace of Tom's arms Serena felt truly disturbed. "I'm not sure that's possible. It'll always be there, Tom. I'll always know that you were the one who broke my father."

Tom's heated glance had nothing to do with passion. "That's the crux of it, isn't it? You refuse to face the truth."

"The truth? *Whose* truth?"

He ignored her barb. "Your father broke himself, Serena. I didn't do it. Oh"—he held up a hand to ward off her protest—"I know what I did. I confess to being impulsive and arrogant. I saw my soapbox and climbed on it with the eagerness typical of a kid. I was young and brash. But though I might have been guilty of zeal, my sense of conviction was intact. I did what I thought was right."

Clutching the sheet to her breasts, Serena rose to a sitting position. "Ruining a man and his family?"

"Standing up for honesty."

"You were ambitious! You were looking for headlines!" Her eyes grew misty. "You didn't care what happened, only that *your* paper got the story under *your* by-line!"

"No, Serena." Tom, too, sat forward, the sheet falling to his navel. "That was a minor point. You didn't know me then. It was idealism as much as anything else that drove me. I was disgusted with what I'd found in that spotlight series of white-collar crime. Your father wasn't the only one exposed."

"He was the only one who mattered to me!"

"I know, I know," he said softly. Lifting a hand, he reached to brush a wisp of hair back from her face.

Serena flinched, her eyes full and luminous. "It's things like *this* that confuse me. How can you be so gentle? . . ." Her words died at the tightening of her throat. How could she be in love? It wasn't right. It wasn't fair. It wasn't possible. Or was it? Tormented, she swayed toward Tom.

"Hold me," she cried in agony. "Make me forget it all, Tom. You can do that." Seeking his strength, she reached tentatively for him.

"Serena, I don't know. . . ."

"Please, Tom." The need was born and swelling fast. "Love me again. Help me."

With a shuddering groan he gathered her to him. "Oh, Serena, Serena. What am I going to do with you? You're as much a split personality as you believe me to be. There's the Strickland side of you that refuses to forgive me for what happened so very long ago. And then there's . . . Serena. Beautiful, sweet Serena. Tranquil to the world, a flame of passion in my arms."

"Tom," she whispered his name against the warm hair of his chest. "Love me . . ."

Knowing he had no choice, his own emotions rising to meet hers, Tom loved her long and hard. This time there were no words of pretense and illusion. There was no slow seduction, no masterful torment. Rather there was the richness of love, raw and new, all-encompassing in its frenzy, and totally beyond control.

The silence of the night was broken only by moans and sighs, by cries of need and gasps of satisfaction. Again and again they sought each other, finding glory in the loss of separate identities, joy in becoming one. There were no attempts at explanation when they fell to the bed a final time, exhausted and weak, yet content. It was as though neither wished to disturb the tentative peace. The light of morning would do that on its own.

Serena awoke to the smell of fresh-brewed coffee and the sight of Tom sitting beside her. He wore nothing but a pair of hip-hugging jeans and an expression that was decidedly troubled.

"I'm sorry." She pushed herself up against the pillows, holding the sheet to her breasts. "You should have woken me sooner. What time is it?"

Returning from the private world of his thoughts, Tom blinked. "It's just after ten. You were tired."

"What about you? Been up long?" She took the mug he had been using when he offered it and sipped the coffee. Its warming effect was secondary to that of the intimacy of sharing.

"Not long. How do you feel?"

She stretched, then blushed. "A little stiff."

"How about a hot shower?"

"Mmm, that sounds good."

"Serena . . ."

"Yes?"

He seemed strangely unsure. "You're free today, aren't you?"

"It's Sunday. The shop's closed."

"No, I mean other things. Can you spend the day with me?"

Looking away, she frowned. "On one condition."

"What's that?"

Her gaze retraced its path to his with deliberateness. "I don't want to rehash that whole thing. Not today." Not after the heavenly night they'd spent in each other's arms.

"Wouldn't it be wise to try to work something out?"

"Not today."

"What good will waiting do?"

Sighing, she closed her eyes and laid her head back against the pillows. "I'm not sure. Put things in perspective? I don't know. It's all bound to hit me when I get back to work tomorrow. I just don't want to rush it."

"You're postponing the inevitable, Serena," he chided, but gently.

"You're right." She grinned, finding strength from some unknown source. "Would you rather take me home now?" The twinkle in her eye was deceptive. Tom saw through it.

"You stay."

"On my terms?"

"On your terms."

"Are you always this agreeable?" she queried in an attempt at lightness. But she hit a raw nerve.

"I'm really not the ogre you try to make me out to be, Serena. I *can* be a nice guy."

Momentarily taken back by the force of his words, she grew sober. "I know that only too well, Tom. And what I'm saying is that I don't want to talk about the ogre today. It's the 'nice guy' I'd like to spend the day with."

As quickly as she'd sparked him she brought a return of pleasure to his morning-fresh features. "The 'nice guy' you've got," he promised, popping a kiss on the tip of her nose before bounding from the bed. "Now, I'd suggest you get yourself into the bathroom while I see to breakfast. Unless," he peered mischievously at her, "you'd rather trade chores."

"No, no. I need the shower." Sitting up, she stopped short, looked around, then down. "Uh . . . Tom?"

"Uh-huh?" Hands on hips, he smiled wickedly.

"I've got one small problem."

"I'll say." The suggestive grin he sent her way spoke of his complete comprehension.

"Well what should I do? I don't really feel like putting that dressy silk thing on again."

Taking pity on her, Tom crossed the room and opened

a closet door, promptly disappearing into an interior Serena hadn't known existed. Leaning forward, she caught sight of shelves and drawers in addition to the standard hanger-laden bar.

"Not bad," she said at Tom's return from the cedar-lined cubicle. "A walk-in closet."

"It holds a world of goodies. Here." Tossing her a large plaid flannel shirt, he continued through to the kitchen. Serena accepted the donation gratefully. Moments later she disappeared into the bathroom.

It was odd, she mused, taking in every detail of the newly refinished room, that the tables seemed to be turned. That first morning, over a month ago, following the more innocent night Tom had spent at her place, he had been the one to make himself very much at home; now she helped herself to towels and shampoo with similar ease. The heat of the shower did wonders for her muscles. The sharp spray drove away the last of the grogginess left by a meager night's sleep. Wrapped tightly in a dark chocolate towel, she stood in delight beneath the overhead heat lamp, combing a semblance of order into her auburn tresses with the gentleness of her slender fingers.

There was a natural beauty about her when she emerged from the bathroom and walked barefoot to the kitchen. Tom was struck instantly.

"Is—is something wrong?" she asked hesitantly.

"Oh, no. Nothing's wrong." His very obvious appreciation underscored that claim. "You look great."

Serena looked self-consciously down at the shirt that fell softly to mid-thigh. She had rolled the sleeves to the elbow and left the collar button undone. As it happened, the second button was sufficiently low to create a decidedly seductive slash from her throat to the swells of her unconfined breasts.

"Maybe I should put the tunic on after all."

"Don't be silly! That's perfect!" In actuality his appreciation was as much for the freckle-studded face, heart-shaped and free of all makeup, with its reckless clusters of auburn waves all about, as it was for the lure of her attire. "Here"—he cleared his throat of its sudden rasp—"have a seat. Brunch is just about ready."

Feeling more confident, she sat before one of the settings he had so carefully placed. "What's on the menu?"

"Nothing exotic—French toast."

"Great! Can I do something to help?"

"No, I'm all set. You just sit and relax. You had a tough workout last night."

Serena propped an elbow on the table, smothered a grimace against her palm and shook her head sheepishly. "That was a cheap shot, but I'll forgive you this once."

Tom's back was to her as he finished at the stove, so she missed his suddenly pensive expression. She did notice that he'd put on a jersey and wondered whether it had been for the sake of warmth or sanity. Either way, she was grateful. The shower had done nothing to purge her of the carnal cravings that his magnificent physique could so quickly stir. It would do well to talk, though. They had both agreed to that.

"I'm sorry I don't have confectionery sugar," he apologized as he put a filled plate before her.

"That's OK. I certainly don't need any. Maple syrup will do just fine." Reaching for the dark brown bottle, she watched Tom settle gracefully opposite her. His eyes studied his own plate.

"It looks prettier with white sprinkles," he commented softly, lost in memories of a favorite childhood meal.

Serena burst into a gay laugh. "You sound so disappointed." Her hand covered his consolingly. "Look at it this way. At *our* age, *neither* of us needs the extra calories. As it is"—she looked helplessly down—"this is loaded!" She took a new tack. "Besides, I see enough sugar coating every day to go without on Sunday."

The smile Tom sent her was devastating. It sent rays of pleasure echoing through her and left a telltale flush on her cheeks.

"Your smile threw me," she confessed on impulse.

"What do you mean?"

"That day in the restaurant when I first recognized you. It was your eyes, their intensity, that seemed so familiar. I knew you from somewhere, but I couldn't place you. Then, at one point, you smiled at your . . . date."

"She's an editor," he corrected her firmly.

"Whatever." It really was irrelevant at the moment. "Your smile is unique, you know."

"So I've been told," he drawled. *That* bothered her more than the thought of the editor she'd seen in person.

"Women must tell you that all the time."

"No. But I have been told so before." He paused. "It's nicer coming from you." He smiled openly at her.

"Ahh . . . you did it again. There it goes. It's very distracting. But I was positive I'd never seen it before. I would have remembered if I had."

Tom grew serious. "You mean that I didn't smile brilliantly in triumph on the day your father was sentenced?" His voice was thick with sarcasm.

Unfortunately, he wasn't far off the mark. She lowered her eyes. "I meant that you never smiled at all during the proceedings. I'm sure you took it all very seriously."

"Thank you."

The silence between them was like a knife cutting into Serena's heart. "Tom, I meant no offense. It was an observation."

Nodding, he concentrated on eating. She studied his bent head. His hair was still mussed from sleep, its gray flecks suddenly more prominent. An odd protectiveness shot through her, making her want to reach out and comb through his hair with soothing fingers.

Needing a diversion, she jumped up. "I think I'll help myself to some coffee. Can I refill your cup?"

"Please." He remained distracted.

By the time she sat down again she felt discouraged. "I don't think this is going to work, Tom." Was bed the only place they could find true compatibility?

"Tell me about *Sweet Serenity.*"

She stared in surprise. "I will, if you stop gritting your teeth."

Her pertness brought a merciful softening to his features. "Am I doing that?" he asked more gently.

"Uh-huh."

"OK, no gritting," he vowed, deliberately relaxing his jaw. "Now, tell me. How did *Sweet Serenity* get started?"

Between juice and coffee and French toast smothered in maple syrup, Serena told the simple story. Engrossed in a subject close to her heart, she felt thoroughly comfortable. Her enthusiasm was hard to ignore.

"It sounds as though Minneapolis has developed a taste for sweets."

She grinned. "It took awhile, but I think we've caused a few addictions. The dental association must love us!"

Tom's answering smile was as fresh and bright as any dentist would have wished. "Dentists may be your biggest fans. For all you know there are a slew of them eating Munch-N-Crunch on the sly."

"Munch-N-Crunch? You remembered! You must have been really observant that day." She recalled her own distraction during the time Tom had been in the shop and wasn't sure whether or not to be offended that his mind had been so free to wander. Reluctant to begrudge him anything at the moment, she chose to forgive him that, too.

"Your stock is original. Very easy to remember. Catchy names. Bright packaging. Personal service. I think you've found the formula for success."

Serena blushed under the praise. "I can't take credit for total originality. Most things come to us with those names. As for the rest"—she shrugged—"it's caught on." Then she paused, suddenly wanting to bounce her idea off Tom. "I'm even thinking of expanding."

"Are you?" he exclaimed, genuinely enthusiastic. "That's great!"

Serena nodded. "*I* thought so. Unfortunately, André didn't quite agree. We were discussing it that day in the restaurant, as a matter of fact."

"What does André have to do with your expanding?"

"He's my investment counselor. For the past few years I've handed over as much of my profits as possible for reinvestment. *If* I decide to go ahead with a branch of *Sweet Serenity* I'll have to withdraw a good sum of the money that André has placed for me."

"He didn't like the idea?"

"Of expansion? No."

"What exactly did he say?"

"He feels that it's premature. That, with the economy and all, I'd be taking too great a risk." She waited for Tom to rebut André's claim. When he didn't, simply continuing to frown deeply, she asked him point blank, "What do *you* think?"

He seemed to grapple with a dilemma. "I don't really know all the facts, Serena. I haven't seen your books."

"But you do know something about the economy. And I'm sure, what with all the investigative reporting you've done over the years, that you've got some kind of a feel for business. Is it stupid to consider expanding into one of the suburbs?"

"Business has been that good in the downtown store?" He eyed her over his coffee, then sipped pensively.

"It's been better than I ever dreamed. In addition, I've gotten into offering services that I never planned on, precisely *because* there's a need. You'd be amazed at the amount of color-coordinated catering I do."

"What the devil is *that?*" Tom looked at her skeptically.

"*That* is when people come in with dishes, bowls, flower pots, decanters, soft sculpture, decorative crystal, you name it, and I fill it with goodies that are color-coordinated with the room in which the piece is to sit. Most people come in before parties. Some come in weekly for standard refills." With Tom now lounging back in his chair, apparently amused by her eager sales pitch, Serena ran helplessly on.

"I never expected to get into corporate work, either, but you wouldn't believe the number of businesses that order custom-made chocolate bars with their logo raised on the front."

"You don't do the actual candy-making, do you?" he mocked in horror. "Somehow I can't picture you standing over a bubbling cauldron with a puffy chef's cap on your head."

The improbable image brought a smug grin to Serena's lips. "Not quite. I've never gotten into candy-making. We have a specialist who takes care of orders like that. As a matter of fact, most of our things are shipped fresh from Chicago."

"You go there often?"

"Not as much as I did at first. It took awhile to get orders straight and pick, by trial and error, the distributors whose goods met the standards I set. Things work pretty smoothly now." She grew more alert. "Which brings me back to the question of expansion. What do you think?"

Tom inhaled deeply, then cast a troubled gaze out the window. "What other capital do you have to work with?"

"Other capital?" she echoed him meekly.

"Don't tell me André's got everything?"

"Just about. I mean, I have some money in the bank for emergencies. But I never had cause to stash any under the mattress, if that's what you're asking. I'm a single woman without dependents. I saw no reason *not* to let André take care of things for me. He came highly recommended."

Tom scowled unexpectedly. "I'm sure."

"What's that supposed to mean?" Did Tom know something she didn't?

"Oh, nothing. I just don't trust the guy."

"I thought you didn't know him. Wasn't last night the first time you two met?" Then she recalled the brief conversation between the two men that had sent her scurrying off to the powder room. "Hmm, he *was* a little offensive there, wasn't he?"

"*You* were more offended than I was." Tom cocked his head and looked closely at her. "Why *did* you get upset like that? Not that I'm sorry, mind you. It was right after that that you asked me to take you away. It seems that André unwittingly did both of us a favor."

Serena wasn't sure enough of the answer to his question even to take a stab. She remembered a feeling of anger, a sense of irritation that André was somehow threatening Tom. Was protectiveness an extension of love? Yet André's caveat had related to the power of the press, its misuse, and subsequent libel actions. Theoretically, given her family's experience, Serena should have sided with André. But she hadn't. Therein lay a poignant message.

"He's not a bad sort." She smiled sadly. "He enjoys a very fast lifestyle and is perhaps a bit too fastidious, but he's a nice guy."

"Then why is he against your expansion?"

With a shrug she offered her own rationalization. "Perhaps he's reluctant to let go of the money I'd need to start the new shop."

"Come on, Serena. I mean, to be honest, he must have plenty of clients who invest far greater sums of money than you do."

"That's what *I* told him."

"And what did he say?"

She recalled how quickly he had changed the subject. "Oh, he kind of made a clever answer and let the matter drop." Her pout fell far short of the indifference she'd intended. It occurred to her that now Tom was overreacting. Was *his* motive protectiveness? Or was he simply emphasizing her questionable judgment in trusting André so explicitly?

"Hmph!" Tom's grunt and its implied disgust would have bothered her far more had it not been for the telephone—it rang, startling them both. "Who the hell could that be? This phone number is unlisted. They know I don't like to get phone calls on Sundays. . . . Hello!" His voice was gruff as he tilted his chair back, the receiver against his ear. Serena was disturbed even before his gaze shot to her. "Yes. This is Reynolds. . . . André?" His tone grew more even, with the barest edge of ice that could only have been detected in contrast to the heat moment before. "How did you get this number? . . . Ah, I might have suspected. . . . Serena? Yes, she's here. . . . Hold on. I'll see if she can come to the phone." The last was drawled on a facetious note and was paired with a gaze tinged with wry humor.

"Are you available?" he asked loudly, making a mockery of his burial of the receiver against the fabric of his jersey. Without hesitating, Serena was beside him, reaching for the phone. But he held it out of reach, forcing her nearer, relinquishing it only when she passed the gates of his knees and stood imprisoned between the iron bars of his thighs. With his ankles crossed behind her she was locked in. A reflexive hand clutched at his shoulder for balance while an impatient one grabbed the phone.

"André!"

She looked down at Tom, he up at her. "Yes, I'm fine."

"Why on earth did you leave like that?"

"Oh, I don't know, André. The party was big and

131

noisy. I just got tired, I guess." She squirmed, aware that Tom's gaze had left her face to study the flesh between the lapels of the flannel shirt. "You got my message, didn't you?"

"Sure, but I was worried."

"There was no need. I'm a big girl."

As though in response to her conversation Tom brought his hands to her shoulders, measuring their slenderness, then seeking other curves. Serena tightened her own hand on his shoulder, but he refused to get the message.

"What are you doing there?" André asked, obviously tempering his agitation.

"Here?" she gulped. "Ah . . . ah . . . Tom was good enough to . . . take me home."

"To *his* home?"

Normally Serena would have had no trouble parrying André's inquiry. It was very difficult, however, with Tom's nearness, the feel of his fingers now dancing at her throat and working their way steadily downward, and the incipient tingling that weakened her knees so that she was grateful for the support of his. Even now she wondered how she could react so quickly to him.

"I was at your house last night," she mustered an argument. "Today I'm here."

"Serena, I've been trying you all night. You haven't been home at all. I finally began calling other people until I found someone who saw the two of you leave together. Very cozy."

Serena closed her eyes and swayed toward Tom, who had very deliberately undone the first of the buttons of her shirt and was working on the next, well aware of the debilitating effect he had on her lucidity.

"André"—she sighed in helpless pleasure at Tom's ministration—"is there something in particular you want?"

"I want to know what you're up to."

132

"That sounds an awful lot like jealousy, André. It doesn't become you. You *know* that there's nothing at all between us." She tried to make her voice as gentle as possible, but it was impossible to hide the shadow of impatience that was caused in large part by Tom's tormenting fingers, wandering now inside her shirt, touching her flesh, creeping along her rib cage to ambush her breasts with devastating accuracy. Arching closer, she moaned a whisper for Tom's ears alone, having the merciful presence of mind to turn the phone away.

"What I really want to do"—André was wrapped up tightly enough in his own world to miss the state of Serena's mind—"is warn you about that fellow."

"Who?" she murmured.

"Reynolds. He's dangerous, Serena. He's a newspaperman."

"I know that." But right now it didn't matter.

"I don't trust him."

"That sounds familiar."

"What?"

"Nothing, André."

"Look, Serena. How about if we meet for lunch. Tomorrow."

Tom had cradled the firmness of a breast in his palm and lifted it to meet his mouth, which enveloped its rosy nub with a heat and moisture that sent her to the far reaches of agonized desire.

"Tomorrow?" Her voice was a weak tremble. "Ah . . . I can't make it."

"Tuesday?" he prodded, while Tom did some prodding of his own, darting his tongue against her other nipple. Sucking deeply, he extracted a sweet sigh from Serena, who held the phone convulsively against her hip.

"Tom," she whispered frantically. "Stop it! I can't think."

"That's the point." He grinned sadistically. "If you can't think, get him off the phone."

In desperation she returned to André. "How about Wednesday? I'll be able to get away then."

He sighed with distinct annoyance. "If that's the earliest you can make it I'll have to settle for it. Wednesday. One-thirty. The usual place. All right?"

She sucked in her breath as Tom's hands scalded the skin of her hips and thighs. "Fine. See you then." She held her breath, praying that André would settle for the date and hang up. Fortunately for her distracted state, he did. It was only when she heard the click on his end and the subsequent dial tone that she collapsed against Tom and let the receiver fall to the floor.

"How *could* you, Tom?" she cried, burying her face in the thickness of his hair. "That was unfair."

"What's unfair"—he tore his mouth from her breasts long enough to argue—"is the softness of your skin beneath my fingers." The digits in question curved around the supple swell of her bottom, coaxing her even closer. "You're so sweet. . . ." His tongue tasted her, leaving hot spots everywhere it touched. She wound her fingers through his hair and forced his head back to stop the torment, but in moments his kiss fanned a red-hot fire against her lips.

Serena had no thought of protest. Tom's every move pleased her beyond imagination. The pain of desire only served to enhance her satisfaction when it came in the form of each deeper foray. They were engaged in an ageless enterprise, though there was nothing of the game in it now. It was for real. And she loved him. Yet she bit her lip to keep from crying it out. The time for confession had yet to come. There was too much to be understood, about him and herself, before those heart's words would be spoken.

A soulful sigh escaped her lips at the willful roaming of Tom's hands. Her entire body was his to explore and he left no niche neglected. "Tom, Tom," she gasped. "What you do to me." Her head fell back to give him access to the sensitive cord of her neck. He gently pushed aside the soft curls of auburn to nibble at her shoulder blade. Cupping his head, Serena pressed him closer, caressing his neck, kissing the crown of his head while his fingers worked hot magic around her navel and across her lower abdomen, down to her thighs and between, intuitively seeking the dark warmth that opened only to him.

Caught once more in the abyss of sensuality, she lost sight of everything except Tom and his body and the driving power of love he inspired. His soft words of pleasure thrilled her in accompaniment to the bold fingers that touched her so tenderly. Crazed with desire, she was barely aware when he shifted her weight to remove the final barriers between them. She knew nothing until seconds later when a hand slid behind each of her thighs to part them and raise them, then positioned her correctly. Slowly, slowly, he guided her down, arching himself to her, moving smoothly as she gasped throatily, her cries bearing the resonance of passion.

"Tom." She panted while he grinned his pleasure at her surprise.

"Didn't expect that, did you?" he murmured.

"No! Oh, Tom . . ."

"Tell me what you want, love." He held himself still, but Serena felt his trembling need of her.

"You. I want you."

His breath came hot against her breasts as his hands stroked the length of her legs curved about his hips. "You've got me, Serena. You've got me."

His lips sought hers in an escape from words. His hands moved to guide her hips. With a heat intense from the start, their momentum picked up with astonishing speed, sending them quickly to the star of fulfillment which sparkled brilliantly, blindingly, before sputtering to a bright shadow, then, finally, a memory.

Arms and legs still wrapped tightly around him, Serena let Tom lift her and carry her back to bed, where they lay spent beside each other in silent awe of what had taken place. They dozed, then awoke and spent the afternoon in easy conversation about a wide range of irrelevant topics. It was only when Serena dressed again in her green silk for the return to her apartment that the name of André Phillips came up.

7

You're going to meet André for lunch on Wednesday?" Tom asked, deep in thought as he absently unlocked her apartment door, pushed it open and held out her keys.

"I think I'd better."

"He was that annoyed?"

A puzzled frown marred the smooth serenity of her features. "Strangely, yes. Though I can't for the life of me understand why." She turned and sank deeply into a chair, leaving Tom still standing. He closed the door, but remained leaning against its frame, all business.

"Perhaps he was miffed that you left without him. After all, he *was* your escort."

"No, it couldn't be that. He knows how I feel—and don't feel—about him. And he was busy enough as host not to miss me." Her auburn waves bobbed gently. "It doesn't make sense."

"Perhaps he was miffed that you left with *me*."

Serena met Tom's gaze head-on. *"That* makes sense.

He's very wary of you." She grinned. "He specifically warned me about you."

Tom's "And rightly he should have!" was growled as he crossed the room to bend over her. "I have an insatiable appetite for sweets." Their lips met in a tasting kiss. All too soon he drew back and straightened. "Tell me, Serena, you're a busy lady. Who the devil are you lunching with on Monday and Tuesday?"

It was the image of innocence that looked up at him. "You," she whispered in a half-question to which Tom chuckled a satisfied reply.

"*That* deserves another kiss." He promptly delivered. It, too, ended too soon to appease Serena's own appetite. "Pick you up at the shop at one?"

"I could meet you somewhere if it would be more convenient," she began, only to be soundly chastened.

"Serena, the next thing I know you'll be insisting we go dutch. Forget it. I'm fetching you at *Sweet Serenity* and treating you to lunch." His good-humored fierceness faded to an endearing plea. "Let me be gallant. OK?"

"OK," she whispered, loving him all the more.

Just as Serena had worried it would, Tom's absence allowed for an invasion of unpleasant and remorseful thoughts. The power of his presence had blinded her blissfully, but without him she was unprotected. His company made her a creature of the present. On her own she was a product of her past, a past in which Tom was a very definite demon.

She was as unable to deny her love for him as she was to foresee any future commitment. Even if Tom loved her he'd been badly hurt once in marriage. Serena questioned whether he would be game to try again.

Game. How satisfying it had been to hear him say that he loved her. Her eyes brimmed in the glow of recollection. But it had all been make-believe. She had to remember that.

Then, of course, there were the Strickland ghosts. In her mind Tom would always be the villain of that debacle. She would forever doubt his actions, perhaps even his motivations. And the weekly Sunday evening call she made to her mother was a further complication. How could she ever, *ever* explain a relationship with Tom to that sad-hearted woman?

Riding on the tail of an uncomfortable sixteen-hour stretch of soul-searching, Serena was wary of what she was doing when Tom entered *Sweet Serenity* Monday promptly at one. She looked sharply up from the customer she was helping, sent him a smile that held its share of tension, and tried to ignore the conflicting thrill of excitement that shot through her at the sight of him.

Tom sensed her tension as though he had expected it. He stood waiting patiently, much as he had done that very first afternoon, until the customer had been satisfied and Serena was free.

"Nancy, I'd like you to meet Tom Reynolds. Tom, this is Nancy Wadsworth." Having made the proper introduction she escaped to the back room to claim her purse, assuming that Nancy would keep Tom entertained for the moment.

Her heart beat quickly, working double-time to integrate doubt and delight. Breathing deeply, she looked down at the hands that clutched the soft leather of her bag. What was she doing? Where was she headed?

"Serena?"

Twirling, she looked shamefacedly up at Tom. "I'm–I'm coming."

The sadness in his eyes spoke of his complete understanding of her plight. "Oh, Serena," he sighed, drawing her gently against the strength of his chest. "I knew this would happen as soon as I left you alone. I bet you didn't sleep at all last night."

"I did. Finally. After all, exhaustion has to take over *sometime*."

"Ever the witty one, aren't you?" He stroked her hair for a moment, then held her back to search her face. "You've been agonizing over it all, haven't you?" After a long, regretful pause she nodded. "I'm sorry, Serena. The last thing I want to do is hurt you."

"I'm all right."

The pad of his thumb caressed her cheek, magnetized by the curve of her lips. "You will be. You're a survivor."

"I try." She spoke softly.

He studied her vulnerable expression and breathed in unsteadily. "I should never have taken you home with me Saturday night. It was wrong of me. I knew what would happen. It's only caused you grief."

Serena smiled her love, aware of Tom's own uncertainty. "I wouldn't say that."

But he needed further reassurance. "Should I stay away? Is our seeing each other just stupid?"

"No!" No matter what doubts she had, the thought of not seeing him was excruciating.

"Then"—he grinned half-jokingly—"I ought to keep you with me all the time. Maybe we should marry—"

"No!" She stumbled at his surprise. "You're no more . . . no more ready for that than I am." It was much too soon for any such thought.

He smiled knowingly, ruefully. "Then what *do* you suggest?"

"Lunch?"

Tom acknowledged her coup with a glance of admiration, then captured her chin with his fingers. "First, a kiss." It was warm and moist, reawakening worlds of pleasure with its simplicity. His lips worshiped hers, moving soulfully against, then with, them. She opened herself to his opiate, let his heady nectar chase away those nagging doubts. When Tom finally and reluctantly released her she was his once more. He sensed his triumph and smiled in victory, but it was a victory they shared. Serena happily took the hand he held out to her and they headed for the plaza.

Having passed that initial hurdle, Serena was as relaxed with Tom as she had been on the day before in the never-neverland of his cottage. He charmed her to the exclusion of all hesitancy; she held nothing back. Over huge deli sandwiches in a tiny restaurant in Cedar-Riverside, where they were afforded the privacy they sought, she regaled him with tales of the occasional business blunders she'd made, most notably the day an irate wife appeared to complain about the order of passion-fruit-flavored jelly beans that had been inadvertently delivered to her house rather than to that of her husband's mistress.

"It was a simple mix-up in addresses," Serena explained with a guilty grin, "but you can be sure I've been more careful since. The husband, my customer, thought he was being terribly clever. He insisted I write the name of the flavor in bold letters on the package. Unfortunately, his wife didn't appreciate it."

"I should think not," Tom chided gently. "That could be very embarrassing for a fellow."

Serena reacted too quickly to catch the humor in his eyes. "It would serve him right! Any husband who blatantly cheats on his wife deserves to be caught. I'd just rather not be the one who's responsible for spilling the beans—no pun intended."

Tom steered the talk toward something that had evidently been on his mind. "Which reminds me, tell me about the men in your life. I got the impression there were quite a few."

Her laughter was light and generous. "You're thinking of that hostess's comment about having to 'wait in line'?" At his look of surprise, she teased him. "I caught it, all right. I may have been distracted that day, but I'm not *totally* thick."

He squirmed in an almost boyish way. "Well?"

"What?"

"Your dates. *Is* there a string of them?"

She lowered her voice. "Jealous?"

"You bet."

"Well, you needn't be."

"Elaborate."

When she feigned distraction and glanced lazily off toward another table Tom reacted with a quick growl. "Serena, tell me about them."

Turning back, she wore a pert smile. "Let me see. First off, there's Greg. He's a lawyer. Kind of like Chocolate Sesame Crunch."

Tom raised both brows speculatively. "Chocolate Sesame Crunch?"

"Uh-huh. Smooth outside, crunchy inside. Pleasant to be with as long as nothing pricks the surface. His inner self is weird."

"That's nice." He smirked.

"Then there's Rod. He teaches psychology at the university." Her hazel eyes hit the ceiling in thought. "He's like gummy bears. Fun and chewy. Too much, though, sticks to the teeth." She looked directly at Tom again. "I'm not wild about gummy bears."

"Thank heaven for that," he muttered under his breath. Serena went on undaunted, thoroughly enjoying her analyses.

"Kenny works at the racquetball club. You may even have met him. I like to compare him to very pretty mint lentils. They're great to pop for quick enjoyment," she informed him in a conspiratorial tone. "Don't look for anything deep in them, though."

"I won't," he drawled, relaxing further. Then he hesitated. "What about me? Have you made a snap comparison?"

Serena stared thoughtfully. "Apricot Brandy Cordials," she announced at last. "Initial judgment, of course. Rich. Sophisticated. With a tang of liquor that can be slightly intoxicating. And sweet. Pleasantly sweet."

"And André? Where does he fit in?"

Though she had never stopped to categorize André before her response was instantaneous. "He's a lo-cal piña colada sucker. He's smooth and cool and tasty. But," she said, seeming almost puzzled, "you get nothing for nothing. He leaves you with a very strange after-taste."

"You may be right," was all Tom said before changing the subject again, apparently satisfied that his competition was no competition at all. And though the matter of André Phillips and the role he played in Serena's life was on both their minds, Tom didn't refer to it again until the next day, when they caught a quick dinner before he dropped her off for her cooking class. Even then, they spent the bulk of the discussion on other, more agreeable topics.

"You never did tell me about your everyday work, Tom," she said, buoyed by the warmth of the embrace he'd given her in the privacy of the small Mercedes before entering the restaurant.

"You're up to it?"

To her own surprise she felt that she was. "I think so. I have to face the reality of what you do sooner or later. And I *am* curious. You don't seem harried like the stereotypical newspaperman."

"I'm not. I *own* the paper. I may write editorials and set policy, but I pay others to meet the deadlines. I make sure they've got the necessary tools and provide them with overall direction, but as for the everyday sweat, it's theirs."

Something melancholy caught her ear. "Do you miss it?"

"The running around—no. I spent over twelve years running. To be blunt, I'm tired. I want to catch my breath, to think, to begin to enjoy the fruits of my labors, so to speak. I paid my dues in the city room; now I've moved on."

"Up," she corrected gently.

He shrugged, as though it didn't matter. "Whatever. I have to admit"—he eyed her with a hint of regret—"that I do miss the excitement of investigation. That's why I—"

When he broke off at mid-sentence Serena prodded. "You what?"

"I like to supervise what the *Bulletin* reporters are doing." He went quickly on. "It's like putting together a puzzle. You fit the border pieces together first, then move carefully and deliberately in toward the heart."

"You sound as much like a detective as a reporter," she said with a shiver as she studied his engrossing hazel eyes and the sense of commitment etched into his features. "I've always wondered at the similarities. Why, for example," she heard herself blurt out, "did *you* get the story about my father before the police did?"

As though afraid of losing her, he took her hand and held it firmly. "There are several reasons, Serena. One is political. Traditionally the authorities have been more hesitant in searching out the white-collar criminal, who may very well have contributed to the campaign chest of the favorite son." He sighed. "Another is practical. The police are bound much more stringently by rules regarding what is admissible in court. If they're doubtful whether they have sufficient evidence to prosecute they may drop the whole investigation, even though they're convinced of a subject's guilt. And then, of course, there's the economic reason. Money. Police departments work within very tight budgets. Newspapers can splurge more often." He held her gaze with an intensity that dared her to turn away from him. "If they hit it big, what they gain in prestige or sales more than compensates for the outlay. Besides"—a grin split his features—"the average investigative reporter doesn't charge time and a half for overtime. Let me tell you, there's plenty of *that* involved. Over the years I came to know intimately the insides of many a library, city hall, and records department."

Serena nodded silently. Why was it that, on Tom's tongue, it all sounded so fair and upright? How could he so easily rationalize what often resulted in such pain for others?

Reading her mind, he answered her question softly. "You have to look at the other side, Serena. The victim. Regardless of what the crime is, there is always a victim. In your father's case the victim was a corporation. In other cases the victims are individuals. In every case someone is hurt, either directly or indirectly." When she still seemed skeptical he ventured further.

"How would you feel, Serena, if *you* were the victim? Supposing, for the sake of argument, that you were ordered to donate $10,000 in cash to the office of a senator or risk losing *Sweet Serenity?*"

"That wouldn't happen."

"It shouldn't, but it could. Schemes like that have been known to take place. If someone threatened to hike your rent so that you couldn't possibly afford to keep the store—unless you made the contribution—how would you feel?"

"Furious!"

"You bet you would. And you'd be justified. Then how would you feel if you went to the police with your story and they refused to do anything? What if they were looking out for their *own* hides? How would you feel then?"

"Furious. Frustrated. Helpless."

"What if *I* then came to you and offered to expose the corruption in my paper. Would you go along with it?"

He'd made his point quite cleverly. It didn't take her long to agree. "Yes, I would."

Tom sensed that he'd given Serena something to

consider, but that he'd said enough on that topic for the moment. Not wishing to dwell on it, yet having good reason, he broached the subject of André. "You're meeting Phillips tomorrow?"

She took a breath to relax. "Yes."

"I wish you wouldn't."

She looked at him askance, nervously mooring her hair behind her ear. "Why not?"

"He may still be angry."

"André? No, he'll have calmed down. If I were to walk into the restaurant with *you* he'd be furious. But by myself I don't threaten him." Tom seemed to contemplate her every word with care. "And anyway, I have to speak to him."

"About the branch store?"

"Yes. If I'm going to go ahead with it I'll need money."

"*Are* you going ahead with it?"

Serena turned the tables, answering a question with a question. "What do *you* think I should do? You never did give me a definite opinion the other day. We seemed to have gotten sidetracked." The flush that accompanied her shy smile brought the memory vividly back into Tom's mind. Beneath the table his hand slid upward on her thigh. Serena felt the instant pounding of blood through her veins. Her only solace was that, if the smoldering fire of Tom's gaze was any indication, her effect on his senses was no less.

"From my very unbiased standpoint," he drawled facetiously, "I think it sounds like a great idea." He sobered fractionally. "If Phillips gives you any guff about handing over the money, let *me* know."

"You'll tie him to the rack on the front page, is that it?" She grinned, delighted at having received Tom's blessing.

"Something like that," he teased, growing bolder.

"Tom!" she cried softly. "This is a public restaurant." Her hand covered his to prevent further mischief, yet she made no move to push it away. Rather, she savored the intimacy of his touch, and let it compensate for the brief chill brought in on the tails of their discussion. *Would André still be angry? Would he persist in trying to dissuade her from expanding?*

At first her worries seemed to have been for naught. When André came forward to meet her the following afternoon he was as warm and chipper as ever. After greeting her with a kiss on the cheek he launched into a dissertation on the glory of the May sunshine and other such pleasantries. Serena indulged him as long as she could. By the time they were well into their luncheon crêpes, however, she felt compelled to touch base on business.

Paving the way for the matter of *Sweet Serenity* and its expansion, she sought to patch up any old wounds. "You're not still angry with me, are you?"

"Angry? With you? No," he drawled with deceptive calm. "I was never angry. I was just worried. Especially when I found out you'd left with *him*."

"What have you got against Tom?"

"I don't like your spending time with him."

"Why not?"

"He makes me nervous. I don't trust him. If it were me, I'd steer clear of him."

Serena couldn't stifle a chuckle. "The two of you sound like little boys in an argument. It's like listening to a recording." Puzzled, she frowned. "And I really can't understand it. Why are you both so wary of each other."

André shrugged innocently. "He's got no reason to distrust me. But *I* know what he is. He's a reporter."

"*Used* to be."

"He snoops into other people's business."

"Now *that* sounds like you have something to hide," she commented lightly.

"Me? Of course not! But reporters have been known

to ruin people. They tend to foam at the mouth when they catch sight of what may be a story. It doesn't matter whether their facts are straight—"

"It does!" she exclaimed with a force she hadn't expected. Quickly she softened her tone. "At least, to Tom it does." André gave her no time to ponder the crux of her admission.

"You've known him for a long time, haven't you?" he took her off guard.

"In a way. Yes and no."

"He came from the L.A. area, just like you did. Were you involved with him then?"

"I was a child then, André. I left the West Coast when I was thirteen."

André nodded, taking in her sudden apprehension. "And what is he to you now?"

The pointed nature of his questions had quickly become offensive. "That's between Tom and me. I don't think it's at all relevant to *us.*" She paused, trying to bring up the subject of expanding as smoothly as possible. "What *is* relevant to us is whether or not I have the money I need to open a branch of *Sweet Serenity.* According to the statements I've received I should have plenty to cover whatever I'll need to get going."

Serena was more disconcerted by the hardening of André's features than she was by his subsequent retort. "You're not still thinking about that, are you? I thought we had agreed to forget about it."

"Not at all," she argued. "I've spent a good deal of time thinking about it and I happen to think the time is right."

"The economy is all wrong, Serena. I told you that before."

"The economy may be shaky, but *I* think *Sweet Serenity* can handle it. Regardless of how tight money is orders are still pouring in. I know that the rent will be high at whatever location I decide on, but I'm convinced that in the long run the store will turn the same kind of profit that the downtown store does."

André was firm, his face set in a mask of civility that belied his inner irritation. "Is Reynolds pushing you into this?"

"Tom has nothing to do with it."

"But he's in favor of it?"

"He agrees with me that it's a good idea. But that's really not the point. *I've* made the decision to go for a second shop. *I* take the responsibility for it."

"Even if it's against my advice?"

Serena was astounded by the vehemence of his warning. She had expected some resistance from him, but not this. "You're my investment counselor, André, not my business manager *or* the chairman of the board. I wish I had your approval; after all, we *are* friends. But it was *my* decision to open *Sweet Serenity* five years ago and it's now my decision to expand."

"It's final then?" he asked, momentarily more sympathetic.

Serena smiled. "Nothing's final until there's a signature on the bottom line. *You're* the one who always tells me that," she teased gently, coaxing him back into a better mood. "I'm going to begin actively looking for locations and figuring out costs from my end. What I'd like is for you to do the same."

"The same?"

"Could you tally up the amount of money I have to work with? My latest statements haven't arrived yet and I have no idea what the dividends will show." When André simply stared silently at her she grew worried. "Is there a problem?"

"No problem." He shrugged too quickly. "When do you want all this?"

"Next week? Same time? Same place?" She tried to make it sound casual in a vain attempt to stem a vague feeling of unease. Mercifully André rose to the occasion, doing one of his characteristic flip-flops, growing instantly charming again. But Serena gave his grave doubts more thought later that afternoon. Much as she tried, she could find no justification for them.

Indeed, she was more determined than ever to go ahead with her plans. The irony of it was that her involvement with Tom, totally aside from the approval he'd given, pushed her on. She had no idea where the relationship was headed, she knew only that the love she felt for him grew by the day. There was still so much to face and work out, though. In that respect, *Sweet Serenity* was her designated diversion. The planning of the new shop would take hours of her time, hours that, should Tom suddenly vanish from her life, would be her key to survival. *Sweet Serenity*, both parent and child-to-be, was her insurance policy for sanity. Through it she had found identity once; if necessary she would cling to it for her life.

"Someone's in love!"

"Excuse me?"

"You heard me, Serena." Cynthia tossed her fire-bright curls back from her cheeks and laughed gaily. "If you could only see your face. You look like a kid caught with her hand in the cookie jar."

Serena's blush approached crimson. "Not quite," she hedged.

"Not quite what? In love? Or caught at it?"

"Not quite either."

"Serena," her friend began as though scolding a child, "you're wearing the evidence, for Pete's sake. It's written all over your face, and you haven't stopped looking around for him since you got here."

"That's not true, Cynthia! He won't be here for at least another hour."

"Ah-hah! So you *are* meeting him here?"

"He's picking me up afterward."

"He's not playing himself?"

"Not tonight. He's got a meeting to attend." Serena bent to lace her sneakers as she recalled Tom's preoccupation when he'd picked her up at work. They had eaten at her apartment before he had dropped her at the racquetball club. His warmth toward her had encouraged her. As always, the doubts that burgeoned with his absence were quickly chased away. But he *had* been distracted; she had sensed something afoot. When she questioned him about it he stilled her with his kiss and the powerful intoxicant of his embrace. She happily pushed aside all worry.

"You *are* in love with him, aren't you?" This time, Cynthia was more serious.

Wrenched abruptly from thoughts of Tom, Serena jerked her head up at her partner, then looked down again to fiddle idly with her laces. She made light of it. "Who knows? Love can blow this way and that. Only time will tell."

Later that evening she feared that time was her enemy. Tom had emerged from his meeting in a shroud of tension that enveloped Serena the instant she set foot in his car. Their conversation during the short drive to her apartment went no deeper than small talk. He was deeply bothered by something, and much as Serena tried to get at its source she could make no headway.

With the panic of a woman in love she concluded that Tom had greater problems with their relationship than she had anticipated. Perhaps there was something more than his failed marriage that tormented him; perhaps there was still a side of him she didn't know. Yet for the first time in her apartment he made love to her and her fears fell victim to the fierceness of his passion. In his arms she knew him well, understanding him and satisfying him with the same fervor he showed her. For those few thoughtless moments they were in harmony. Soon after it was shattered.

8

I've done some thinking about your plans for *Sweet Serenity*," Tom began as they lay in bed together, her head nestled on his shoulder. "Maybe you ought to wait before opening a second store."

"*What?*" Serena bobbed up in surprise, but he pressed her back with a determined hand and held her there.

"The branch store. Why don't you wait a few months?"

"What difference would a few months make?"

She felt his shrug beneath her head. "Rents may have leveled off by then, money may be that much freer."

"Do you really believe that, Tom? Do you really think a few months will reflect a turn in the economy?" She offered soft skepticism.

"Never can tell." His nonchalance was more than she could bear, particularly given her doubts of earlier that evening.

"I don't understand," she argued in a hurt whisper.

"You were in favor of the idea when we discussed it the other day. Why have you suddenly changed your mind?"

"I haven't changed my mind about expanding per se. I'm simply suggesting that you may want to wait before taking such a large step. It may be premature."

"I can't stand it!" she exploded, overpowering him and sitting up. "Now you sound like André! What is it with you two?" Her gaze narrowed. "Who *was* your meeting with tonight, anyway? You were pretty vague about it before."

Tom stroked her arm slowly. "It was a matter relating to the paper, Serena. I can assure you, I've had no meetings with André. The incident at his party was enough to persuade me to keep him at arm's length. I only wish you would."

"He controls my money, Tom. I can't very well avoid him. And besides, I still don't see what you have against him."

Tom said nothing, simply reached up to twist an auburn wave through his fingers. His eyes—those fire-laden eyes—held an enigmatic blend of gentleness and anger. Serena was totally confused.

"This is absurd!" She finally cried out her frustration. "The two of you seesaw and I'm stuck in the middle sliding first one way, then the other."

"It's not that way. At least, I had hoped that I had the greater weight of emotion on my end."

With a sigh of helplessness at the beseeching look in his eyes she let her arms rest on his chest, then slowly settled down on its solid expanse. She breathed in the musky scent of his skin. "Oh, Tom, you know you do. It's just that, well, *Sweet Serenity* is my passport to security. It means the world to me. Expansion is something I've been considering for a while now. Perhaps I'm worried that if I put off the move I may get cold feet myself."

He held her quietly, ingesting her words, his arm

circling her ivory-sheened back. "You're a very stubborn lady," he admitted at last, "but I suppose it's one of the things I like about you. You're committed to this, aren't you?" She nodded, rubbing her cheek against the dark mat of hair just below his throat. "Just promise me one thing?"

"Hmm?"

"If Phillips gives you trouble, let me know?"

Startled, she looked up again, only to be beset with perplexity when her memory dredged up a similar warning that Tom had given her last weekend. It was as though he actually expected André to present a problem, and that was the last thing she anticipated. Wary, and feeling as if she had missed a vital clue, she sought to reassure Tom once more.

"I'm sure there won't be any trouble, Tom. André was hesitant at first, but that was only natural. He expressed the same doubts you just did. But I seem to have convinced him. We're meeting next week to discuss specifics. He'll have the figures with him, plus papers for me to sign. I have to say that he was a gracious loser." She paused and studied Tom's frown for a minute longer before a saucy smile toyed with her lips. Drawing her leg up along the man-roughened length of his she lowered her voice to a whisper. "What about you?"

To her delight the frown evaporated into the late May night as Tom's lips found hers in a final impassioned seal of affection before he reluctantly hauled himself from the bed and dressed. It was amid promises of a weekend together that Serena mustered the strength to let him go, her spirits high in anticipation.

They dined in elegance Friday night following a performance at the Guthrie Theater. For Serena, however, the highlight of the evening was the return to Tom's cottage and a night of bliss spent in his arms. When she impishly told him so he grinned and kissed her before urging her to sleep.

155

He drove her to *Sweet Serenity* on Saturday morning, then brought in roast beef sandwiches for three at noon, automatically including a noticeably star-struck Monica in the trio, putting her gently at ease. For the first time since opening the shop Serena would have liked to have taken the whole day off to be with Tom. But his acceptance of her obligation and his very evident admiration of her dedication compensated for his absence, temporarily appeasing the addiction she now freely admitted to herself. When he reappeared at six to pick her up she felt the familiar surge of excitement.

Even the brief stop at her apartment for a change of clothes was more than Serena would have wished. She breathed a sigh of relief when the sturdy oak door of the small brick cottage closed behind them, excluding the world and its worries from their utter intimacy. Here she felt free of all care. Here she blossomed as a woman in Tom's hands, letting the love she felt be contained only by fear of confession. For though his behavior and the very way he looked at her bore all the warmth she might have hoped, he spoke no words of love.

In her way, despite the strength of her own emotions and the love she felt for Tom, Serena was grateful. There were still those fleeting gremlins of doubt flickering through her mind at idle, solitary moments. Until the last of these was banished she was no more ready for commitment than was he.

The first part of the week flew by with hardly a moment's breather. Not only was there the routine functioning of *Sweet Serenity* to oversee, but Serena's sights were set on the future. Leaving Nancy to man the store for several hours each day, she made a whirlwind tour of available rental spots in the communities surrounding Minneapolis, communities she had previously targeted for potential branch stores. In the end there were three viable possibilities, any one of which would have pleased her.

Armed with a folder of facts, figures, and statistics, she met André as arranged. It was with mixed emotions that she submitted to his warm hug in the foyer of the restaurant, then let him rest his arm on her shoulder as they walked to their table. Much as the open, and shallow, display of affection bothered her, she felt she was in no position to offend André by making an issue of it. She was grateful enough for his good mood to overlook the indiscretion.

Over the course of the meal they discussed the details of Serena's plans. She produced sheet after sheet of projected expenses, relying on André's friendship more than his occupation, under which such duties did not traditionally fall, to guide her. He listened to her presentation with a positive concentration that encouraged her so much that when, at last, he withdrew a sheaf of papers from his own pocket she readily signed her name to the consent form allowing André to retrieve her money on her behalf without stopping to read carefully through it. When he promptly pocketed the form and leaned forward to excuse himself from the table for a moment she sat back with a decidedly satisfied air.

As the seconds ticked away, however, her satisfaction thinned. It had been too easy; André had been too agreeable. Considering the force of his opposition at the start of their discussion last week, his unquestioning cooperation seemed odd. Or, she asked herself in an attempt to be fair, had Tom merely planted the seeds of doubt in her mind? Perhaps all was well. But where was André?

Rather than abating, her apprehension grew at the sight of him walking confidently toward her. For in contrast to the benign smiles he had bestowed on her earlier, his expression now held the same hardness she had seen last week. Then he had persisted in fighting her intent; what now? It had all been decided; she had given him her instructions to see about withdrawing her capital.

Then it suddenly occurred to her that André had not yet shown her the full figures on her accounts. As he sat down she stiffened slightly.

She picked up where they had left off before André had smoothly pocketed the release form. She struggled to keep her voice nonchalant. "Is everything all right?"

There was an insidious tilt to his smile. "Everything is fine," he reported, downing the last of his wine and facing her boldly. She felt instinctively that they were talking about totally different things.

"When will I have access to my money?" she asked, barely concealing her timidity behind a skillfully smooth facade.

"It will be a while."

"A while? Is that days . . . weeks?"

"It's hard to tell, Serena. I'll let you know as soon as I learn anything."

"André, I don't understand. I thought that I would be able to get my funds within days, no *more* than a week."

"Times are tight."

"It's *my* money." She frowned, tempering her growing irritation. "By the way, have you got some figures for me? I haven't seen the tally you were going to make. I'm not even sure exactly how much we're talking about."

He didn't blink. "I'm still working on putting the figures together. I'll get back to you on it." A smile that was intended to pacify her missed its mark entirely.

"You're putting me off, André," she accused softly.

"Of course not, Serena. Everything will be taken care of in due time." He patted her hand as though she were a pet, angering her all the more. "Just be patient."

"But I'm ready to go. There doesn't seem to be a point in delaying, unless you have some other reason . . . ?"

"Patience."

Taking a different approach, Serena withdrew her hand from the tablecloth, tucked it tensely inside the other on her lap and took a deep breath. "André, what's going on? Something is very strange here. You remind me of the salesperson who's full of smiles when a sale is made, and all but cursing you when you bring the item back because it doesn't fit properly. We're friends. I don't quite understand your attitude."

Neither did she understand the glitter of power that his eyes held, nor his seeming indifference to her concern. "Don't push it, Serena," was all he said through a brightly pasted smile.

"André . . ."

"Don't push!" He grew abruptly sober, as though she had, with her gentle prodding, offended his pride and cornered him.

Serena was totally confused. What puzzled her most was the sense of inevitability in what was happening. "André, you *do* have the money I gave you to invest, don't you?" She spoke on impulse as the terror of suspicion entered her mind. Was it possible that something *had* happened to her nest egg, and that he was afraid to tell her for fear of upsetting her? But she was upset enough as it was. Now she wanted the truth. She was stunned into silence by what André had to say.

"I know about you and Reynolds, Serena."

"*Wh—what?*"

The venal narrowing of his gaze sent a shudder of fear through her. "I went way back to the time you lived in California. You left with quite a bang, didn't you?"

Serena blanched, staring at him with every bit of the disbelief she felt. Forgotten was the lovely atmosphere, the hum of chatter all about them, the many pleasant times they'd shared as friends. She could only focus on his words and their vicious implication.

"What are you talking about, André?"

"Your father." He stared hard. "I know about your past."

She held her breath for the half-minute it took her to recover from the first of the shock. "Yes, well . . . what does that mean? What difference does it make?" Hadn't Tom told her that *she* was the only one to whom that long-ago trauma was meaningful? Evidently he was wrong.

The gleam in André's eye spoke of the pleasure he received from her vulnerability. "I knew there was something odd in the way you looked at him that day." His voice was low, his mind raging in its own direction. "Reynolds was the one who exposed your father. The newspaper files had it all, right there in black and white."

She could only swallow hard and repeat her earlier question. "But what does that mean? I know what's there. But I don't see that it has any relevance to what you and I are talking about. All that happened sixteen years ago. My father paid for what he did. It has nothing to do with my plans for *Sweet Serenity.*"

"I hope it won't have to."

The hollow in her stomach gaped with the lethal calm of his voice. "André!" she cried, exasperated and confused. At his warning glance around, a reminder of the public nature of their surroundings, she dropped her voice to a more cautious pitch. "I can't believe this! I must have missed something somewhere along the line. Why don't you explain it to me?" Her appeal was to the friendship they had shared once, but it fell on ears to which that friendship apparently meant nothing.

He sat forward, smiling for appearance's sake. His tone held neither humor nor sympathy. "All right, Serena, though I had thought you were quicker. Let me spell it out. I can't give you your money now and I won't be pressured. If need be I can easily spread word about your family's history. That might make it more difficult for you to find a landlord willing to rent to you."

Horrified, she could only take one thing at a time. "Wait a minute. Let's backtrack here. You say you *can't give me my money now?* Why not? I thought that every investment you made for me had a clause concerning withdrawals—"

"They may have."

"Then, why . . .?" With understanding came even greater dismay. "It's gone . . . you've done something with it . . . how *could* you?"

"I've done things I thought would work out. I just need more time. You'll have your money, Serena."

"When? This isn't fair! I need that money if I hope to open—"

"I've already advised you against expansion at the present."

"And I can see why!" Furious, she had to lower her voice again. "How could you do this to me? How could you do it to *any* client?"

The slightest flicker of remorse appeared in André's eyes, then vanished with a return of his rock-hard expression. "I have my own pressures, Serena. It's not easy to support my ex-wives, the children, the house in Kenwood, and my other expenses. I've simply used your money—"

"—only mine?"

"Yours and *others'* money, to make different kinds of investments. They've been slightly more speculative. I'm waiting for them to pay off. Then I can return your money to you." A fine line of sweat just above his lip belied the calm tone of his voice.

"And you honestly think you'll hit it big?"

He tilted his head in a cocky manner. "I don't see why not. It's just taking longer than I had expected. Actually, I hadn't thought you would want to use that money so soon."

Serena's gaze leveled in anger. "It's theft, André. You know that, don't you?"

"I like to call it borrowing."

"Call it what you will, it's a crime—"

"—about which *you* will do absolutely nothing!"

"How can you be so sure?" she asked. "Do you know what that money meant to me, André? Even aside from the matter of a second store, it was the bulk of my savings. I'm on my own. I don't have anyone looking out for me. I don't have an inheritance coming to me. That's my future you're playing with, and I don't like it! What I've given you over these past few years may be less than what some of your other clients have, but to me it's a large sum. I can't believe you'd do this to me, André! I can't believe it!"

André seemed indifferent to the hurt in her eyes. "I'm sorry, Serena," he offered impassively. "All I can say is that you *will* get your money. Sooner or later."

She drew herself up stiffly in her chair. "You bet I will!" Though she had no particular plan in mind she knew she had to do something. As the victim of such a cold-blooded scheme she was incensed.

André, however, anticipated her. "Don't do anything, Serena. Remember, I know everything."

Her breath caught and hung in her throat. He *did* know and the determined set of his features said that he would indeed use anything and everything against her. "You really would hurt me, wouldn't you?" she finally choked out, struggling to think straight.

"Reluctantly, Serena." He reached out to take her hand, but she snatched it away quickly. André was undaunted. "You know how I feel about you—"

"It won't work!" she lashed out. "You can't hurt me with your stories."

"They're not just stories, Serena. You know that. The papers were quite specific about both the charges and the conviction."

"That's history. I have my own life now."

"You're right." He smiled smugly. "You've got that very sweet little shop of yours. Your customers adore you. They think you're the very image of innocence. It would be a shame if they discovered that your father was a convicted felon."

The knot in her stomach had spread, leaving her pale and taut. "You really would try to destroy me, wouldn't you?"

"Only if you force me to. Actually, there's no reason why we can't make an agreement."

"What kind of agreement?"

"It's very simple. You bide your time on the second store until I cash in on my profits. I'll even give you an added bonus. Call it interest."

"That's disgusting! I don't want any of your money, I only want mine."

He shrugged. "I'm sorry."

In that instant Serena made a decision. Where she found the strength she would later wonder, but there was no hesitation in her voice when she called André's bluff. "I'll expose you, André. This isn't fair. I trusted you, gave you practically every extra cent I made on the shop. What you've done is criminal."

"You won't expose me."

She shook her head. "Don't threaten me again. It won't work. You can go ahead and spread any story you want. My family paid years ago for what my father did. I refuse to pay now. I've worked too hard in the past five years. The reputation of *Sweet Serenity* can stand on its own."

It had been her hope that André would back down under the threat of his own exposure, even offer to retrieve whatever funds he could for her. When he simply reached into his pocket, put before her the same sheet of paper she had signed earlier and leaned complacently back in his chair she froze.

"What's this?"

"Read it."

"It's the paper I just signed. A release for you to withdraw my funds."

"Read it."

Trepidation shot through her as she lowered her eyes to the paper. At once she knew it was different. Whereas the piece of paper she had signed had been set in the standard form of a release, this was a letter. The only thing that was the same was her name, signed in her own hand, at the bottom.

She was overwhelmed with confusion, then disbelief, then fear as her eye moved from line to line, slowly down the page. Blood thundered through her veins, reverberating throughout her body, amplified in her head. When at last she put the letter down and looked up she was dazed.

"I don't believe this," she whispered. All the color had drained from her face. Her hazel eyes were suddenly hollow.

André could as easily have been telling her about his plans for the weekend for all the nonchalance of his declaration. "You'd better believe it, Serena. What you have before you is a letter that implicates you in everything I've done."

Her voice wavered. "It does more than that and you know it."

He smiled. "So you did get the gist."

"It not only proclaims my involvement, but implicates *me* as the mastermind!" Appalled, she looked down again. "But this is false! I never signed anything like this!"

"That's your signature," he said, enjoying his feat.

"Yes, I know. But I didn't put it here . . . on this piece of . . . trash. . . ." Taking the paper, she waved it in the air.

"I'd warn you to be careful, but that's only a copy. I have another safely tucked away." He patted his breast pocket.

Serena was still stunned. "How did you . . . my signature . . ."

"Very simple." He grinned, leaning forward with pride. "The *top* paper, which *you* signed, was the standard release you thought it was. *Underneath* was the letter you're holding."

"Then this is a carbon . . . ?"

"Can't tell the difference, can you?"

Peering closely, she studied her signature. To her chagrin she couldn't see any difference. It looked exactly like the original. "No one would believe this . . . this nonsense."

"Anyone who knows of your past would believe it in a minute."

"How could you!"

"Now, now." He squeezed her hand. She was too dismayed to move it. "Keep your voice down. We've got lots of witnesses. Witnesses to our frequent luncheon dates. Same time. Same place. Witnesses to a hug here, a kiss on the cheek there. For all outward purposes we could be lovers."

"Heaven forbid!" she spat out with the thrust of the horror she felt. "This won't work!"

"Are you going to put it to the test?"

He had very deliberately hit on the crux of the matter. *This* was his bluff; did she dare call it? On the one hand, if his threat held up, she would face the loss of her shop, perhaps worse. On the other, she would simply have to postpone plans for expansion. He might even come through with her money eventually. Otherwise she would have to accept its loss.

Either way, her choice was a poor one. And, in the state of emotional upset to which his well-plotted scheme had reduced her, she couldn't make the decision. Without another word she clutched her bag, rose from her seat, and headed for the door. André, however, caught her hand as she passed and stopped her short. In the same fluid movement he rose to stand beside her. The pressure of his fingers ensnaring hers contrasted sharply with his outward show of control, which in turn masked the venom of his low warning.

"I'd think about it carefully, Serena. You have everything to lose." He bent toward her ear. The faint tug of his arm held her in place. "And I wouldn't go to Reynolds with this, if I were you. He'll blurt your admission all over page one. And, after all"—he straightened—"I have *my* reputation to consider."

Serena's body felt suddenly chilled. "Tom wouldn't do anything to hurt me."

"For your sake, I hope not. But his business is newspapers, Serena. He gave you a good example of his power back in Los Angeles. I wouldn't trust him, but then, I've told you that before, haven't I?"

His taunting leer revived her anger. "You're a snake, André. A snake. And you *will pay* for this, so help me."

"Don't make threats you can't keep."

In a burst of fury-driven strength Serena tore her hand from his and made for the exit, refusing to look back, holding her body steady, her head high. She was unaware of the beauty of the fine spring day, oblivious of the gay flowers that had materialized by the trees far below in the plaza. She looked nowhere but forward until she reached *Sweet Serenity;* only then did the enormity of André's threat hit her. It was nothing short of blackmail, but, for the life of her, she didn't know how to fight it. She had worked so hard to make a success of her life. Now because of a tragic misplacement of trust, she risked losing it all. She retreated into the back room to consider her alternatives.

"Another headache, Serena?"

"Oh, Monica!" Serena twirled around to face the young girl. "Yes, I do have one. It's not too bad, though. Perhaps you could cover for me up front?"

"Sure. Is there anything I can do?"

"No." Serena shook her head sadly. "I think I'll just take care of some of these things." Her gaze blindly skimmed the throng of sacks and cartons. "You go on out there. I'll be fine."

Monica promptly disappeared, leaving Serena alone with her fears. It seemed an insurmountable problem. Could her past really have come to haunt her this way?

Her eyes suddenly filled with tears. Had Tom been wrong, after all? Was she destined to be forever tormented by what her father had done so long ago? But, no, Tom had *not* been wrong on those other things. *He* had been wary of André all along. *He* had questioned her putting all of her eggs in one basket. *He* had justified his own actions as a reporter by forcing her to picture the anguish of victimization. Now it was no picture. It was real. Fact. And she finally understood the pain of the true innocent, for it was hers.

"Serena?"

Startled from her fog, she glanced up at Monica. "Yes?"

"There's a phone call for you—Mr. Reynolds."

Throat choked with anguish, Serena simply shook her head and waved a hand to indicate that she couldn't talk. Whatever could she say? One part of her—the part that was filled with fury—wanted Tom to do just what André had suggested he *would* do, to splash headlines over page one of the *Bulletin,* decrying a crime in the process. But such a headline would surely incriminate *her,* rather than André. *He* had covered his steps quite nicely.

Monica reappeared through a mist at the door. "He'd like you to call him back when you're free."

Serena nodded, then immediately ruled out that possibility. This was not Tom's battle; it was hers. She could not face the hypocrisy of running to him for help after she had accused him of using his paper for gain. What was the alternative? Could she go to the police? But what if they believed André? What if the police decided that she *had* been the mastermind of the entire scheme? *What if Tom believed it as well?*

It was this last thought that shook her the most. When he called a second, then a third, time she refused to take his calls. Knowing that she'd taken the route of the coward, she also knew that she needed some time to think. She still had the option of going along with André's directive, of remaining silent and simply waiting for her money. But what about her hopes? Her plans? Her dreams of security and self-sufficiency if the money was lost?

She steadied herself, fighting to control rising panic, struggling to contain the headache that throbbed loudly. Time. She needed time. But when Tom stormed into the shop shortly after five she knew that time had run out.

9

〰〰〰〰〰〰〰〰

Where is she?" His voice resounded from the front of *Sweet Serenity* to its back, where Serena stood carefully unwrapping a delivery of delicate crystal decanters. Her hands trembled as she placed the one she held back into its box; then she hung her head in defeat. "Serena?" His voice was closer, louder, filled with an anger that was miraculously mixed with concern. "Serena!"

She didn't look up to admire the way his manly frame filled the door or how handsome he looked in his customary blazer and slacks. All that was inscribed on her mind's eye; her own would merely blur the image.

"Serena?"

Had he yelled in anger she might have been able to put him off. But the exquisite tenderness in his tone was her undoing. Covering her face with her hands, she began to cry softly.

"Oh, Serena." He was beside her in an instant, pulling her toward him, into the sanctuary of his embrace. "What is it, Serena? Please tell me." But she couldn't speak, and simply clung to him. And he held her tightly, waiting patiently for her to regain her composure.

"You shouldn't have come," she finally gasped against his shirt, fingering the moisture left by her tears.

"Like hell I shouldn't have! When you refused to take or return my calls I got concerned. And it's a good thing I did!"

"No, you don't understand." Pushing from his grasp, she looked up, unaware that her fingers pressed her eye to still the throbbing just above it.

He took one look at her. "Damn! Come on, we're leaving." He looked around for her bag at the same time that he curved his fingers firmly about her arm.

"I can't leave now, Tom! There's still another hour before closing time!" Her whisper held the ragged remnants of weeping.

Tom's voice was softer, more understanding. His eyes held incredible warmth as he brushed at her tears with his free hand. "Monica can take care of things here. She can close up for once. You've got a headache, and your medicine is at home. Right?"

Through her misery she nodded. "But Monica's never closed up before."

"There's a first time for everything. She'll do fine. If there are any problems she can call me and I'll come back here to help. Now, do you need anything besides this?" He had somehow found her pocketbook in the array of goods surrounding them.

Serena shook her head. "Really, Tom . . ." But she felt worse than ever and broke off her own protest. It seemed that history repeated itself. Such a short time ago Tom had invaded her world, coming to the shop that afternoon, taking her home that evening, caring for her in a way that had sown the seeds of love. Now she understood the fullness of her love, *and* the awesome mess she was in. Somehow a dose of medicine sounded very much like a makeshift solution. Evidently Tom agreed.

"I'll take you home; you can take a pill and lie down. After an hour or so, when you're feeling better, I want you to tell me what's bothering you." His order was given only after he'd helped her into the Mercedes. By that time she had acclimated herself to the idea of leaving *Sweet Serenity* for the day. Spilling all her problems to Tom was another matter, but one she couldn't contemplate through the incapacitating thud in her head.

By car her apartment was two minutes from the shop. Before she was even able to suggest that Tom leave her and come back another time he had taken her hand and led her inside, guiding her into the elevator and up, opening the door for her and ushering her in. Through it all she kept her eyes downcast, to ward off the pain.

Last time she had staggered alone to her bedroom; this time Tom was by her side the whole way, leaving her only to get her pill and some water, returning to help her undress and get into bed. This time he stayed in her room, keeping guard in the darkness, waiting for her revival. As before, she buried her head against the pillow, dozing as the medicine went to work. When she awoke, however, her hand was in Tom's and he sat close beside her, stroking her hair with infinite tenderness. To her chagrin she started to cry once more.

"You—you should go," she stuttered in muffled misery.

"I'm going nowhere." To emphasize his determination he bodily lifted her and set her against him as he leaned back against the headboard. "Now, cry if you want, but get it out of your system. I want to hear what happened today to upset you like this."

"Oh, Tom, it's such a mess. You don't want to hear . . ."

"Would you rather I rushed out of here and took my fury out on André Phillips?"

Her whisper was weak. "André?"

"Yes, André! I know you had lunch with him today. And, according to Monica, you were upset from the minute you returned. Now, will *you* tell me what happened—or do I go to *him?*"

Much as she needed the comfort of his nearness, Serena pushed herself away and sat up. "I'd like to wash my face. I feel terrible." Without waiting for his approval she threw on her robe and fled to the bathroom, emerging after a short time feeling no better for the cold water she had thrown on her burning cheeks. She walked to the refrigerator, where she helped herself to a tumbler of iced water, then looked up to find Tom following her every move.

"Would you like to wash the floor and clean the oven before we get down to this?" he drawled facetiously. "Or do you think we can finally talk?"

Serena escaped past him to the living room. "There's really nothing to say." She hugged her middle with one hand, her chilled glass with the other.

"I can't imagine that anything's happened between *us* to upset you; you were happy enough last night."

"It's nothing to do with you."

Tom had advanced and now stood tall behind her. "Then it has to do with our friend, the money man. Are you going to tell me what he said when you met with him today?"

"It's not important."

"Like hell it isn't! It was enough to keep you from speaking to me this afternoon. Tell me, Serena!" She simply shook her head and looked down. "Then, I'll call him."

"No!" She whirled around, oblivious of the water sloshing on the rug.

"Then you tell me."

"I can't!" Her voice was higher with each protest.

"Serena . . ."

"No!" she screamed, then again, "No! I can't take any more threats. Don't push me into a corner, Tom! I don't think I can bear it!"

With deliberate calm Tom took the glass of water from her hand and put it safely on the mantel. His fingers cupped her chin and tipped it up until she had no choice but to look at him. What she saw stirred every bit of the love she felt and she trembled anew.

"If there's something wrong, Serena," he spoke slowly, softly, "I want to know."

"It's *my* problem," she began in a whisper, only to be jolted by the quiet vehemence of Tom's correction.

"It's *our* problem. Haven't you learned that yet? It's *our* problem, Serena."

Still her protesting whisper persisted. "I can't run to you with my burdens, Tom. I can't just dump them on you. It's not fair!"

He hesitated for a split second before voicing thoughts that had been held off for too long. "Is it fair that I love you?" he murmured achingly, bringing both hands up to frame her face. "Is it fair that, after everything I did to your family years ago, I expect that you might love me back? Is it fair that I've finally found what I've searched for all these years, only to have it kept away by a ghost from the past?"

Serena couldn't believe the words Tom spoke, but they were reinforced by the gentleness of his touch and the devotion in his eyes. They were words she had wanted so badly to hear; she should have been ecstatic. Why, then, did she feel an overwhelming sense of fear? Was the greatest hurdle still ahead?

Her hazel eyes widened as she stared at him. Her words were choked when she forced herself to speak. "I don't know what to do."

For what seemed an eternity of silent communication Tom read in her eyes the message of her heart. "Do you love me?" he whispered at last. When she nodded, his hands tightened by her ears. "Then trust me. Please. That's the only way we can see through this. Trust me. Trust me to be able to help you, to do what's right. If you can't do that we have no hope."

"I want to trust you, Tom. You have no idea how much. And I do. It's just that . . . I feel so . . . helpless."

Leading her gently toward the sofa, he sat her down, then knelt before her. "All right, honey. Now, I want you to start from the beginning. It's got to do with Phillips, doesn't it?"

She nodded, then slowly gathered the strength to tell him everything. She held nothing back, counting on the force of his love and the trust she felt to overcome any doubts either of them had. When she had finished relating the course of her meeting with André she hesitated, noting Tom's deep concentration. "You must think I'm a fool for getting into this mess."

Her vulnerability snapped him from his preoccupation. He moved to sit beside her and drew her against him. "I think you're a fool for not having called me the minute you got back to the shop after lunch. What ever possessed you to keep this to yourself?"

Her words were muffled against his chest, but she answered him anyway, suddenly needing for him to know everything. He was right; if there was to be any hope for their love only the complete truth would do.

"I felt ashamed, for one thing."

"Ashamed? Honey, he's a scoundrel. If it wasn't you it would have been someone else. And from what you say, there *are* others whose funds he's used."

"But you warned me. And I didn't listen."

"It was just a hunch on my part then. This is the first piece of concrete evidence we've got against him."

There was a greater meaning to his announcement than Serena was able to assimilate at that moment, so intent was she on telling him all. "But it would have been hypocritical for me to run to you and expect you to publicly expose him after I'd held you at fault all those years for exposing my father like that."

"Serena," he murmured against the warmth of her hair, "I was overzealous way back then. I've never regretted exposing a crime, though I have agonized over my methods. I've mellowed, I suppose. We'll deal with André in a different way."

"You do believe *me* then?"

"What?" He held her back to study her fear. "Did you honestly think I might not?"

"Well, after all, I am the daughter of a convicted felon."

"Serena! When are you going to be able to forget that? I'm in love with you because you're sweet and sincere, innocent and warm, brimming with bundles and bundles of love. I don't give a damn who or what your father may have been. It's you I love! You!" Short of taking her by the arms and shaking her he couldn't have made his point more forcefully. The fire she knew so well was in his eyes. It was the fire of love.

His kiss held the promise of a future filled with that same fire. She returned it eagerly, gaining faith with each caress and hope with each soft-whispered vow of love. All too soon he held her back to look at her. Satisfied that the worst of her torment was behind, he set about working to eliminate the rest.

"I'd like to see the paper André gave you. Have you got it?"

"I certainly do." Without hesitating she retrieved it from her purse and handed it over to Tom.

He studied it closely, turning to catch the light at different angles. When he looked up, there was taut-held fury in his gaze. "That swine. He thought he could blackmail you with *this?*"

Serena frowned, then brightened at his implication. "You mean it *won't* pass as an original?"

"To the naked and untrained eye, perhaps. To an

expert, no way. Unless André produced an original he'd never have a case."

"The original *was* a standard release form. He told me that. And I'd bet that he tore it up and flushed it down the pipes when he went to the men's room. He was in an unnatural rush. But, Tom, the only way we can prove anything is if we go to court! I don't want it to come to that!"

Seeing her distress, he took her hand. "It's not going to go that far. André is bluffing; you know that. And, innocent that you are, you didn't call him on it and make it stick any more than you called me on my bluff that first day when I really didn't remember who you were." Leaning forward, he pressed a gentle kiss to her lips. "I do love you." He smiled, shaking his head at the wonder of it. "And I do want to protect you. Do you know that that was the very first thing I felt that day in the restaurant? There was such hurt in your eyes when you looked at me. I didn't know who you were, only that I somehow wanted to protect you. Little did I know that your fear was of *me!*"

Entranced by his fierce tenderness, Serena wove her fingers through the hair by his temples and brought him forward for another kiss. Her lips were a warm breath of femininity on the male-firm contours of his, speaking of her own adoration with startling aggressiveness. Needing to know of her love, Tom held up his response, forcing from her a most glorious statement, written by her lips, underscored by her tongue, and backed by the way she opened completely to him. With a low moan he yielded to her power, succumbing to the golden glow she cast over him.

"Serena," he groaned, "we've got to stop this. There's so much to figure out." Panting, he sat back. "I could make love to you all night, but that won't do anything to solve this problem with André. Let me think." Knowing his withdrawal to be in her own best interests, Serena moved further back on the sofa and tucked her feet under her. The dilemma with André hadn't eased in the least, yet knowing that Tom would share in the solution brought her great reassurance. She believed in him. She trusted him. Together they would work something out.

Together they did work something out. Or, rather, Tom did, for Serena remained confused, largely in the dark, following his directives without quite understanding the power of the punch line.

She had some doubts when she put through a call to André that evening, claiming that she wanted to talk again, even offering to cook him breakfast the next morning. Made complacent both by the note of fear in her voice and the state of his overblown ego, he accepted her invitation.

She had further doubts when Tom left her for a short time that night, returning under cover of darkness with armloads of recording equipment and one plainclothes detective who quite casually spent the night on the sofa while Tom shared Serena's bed.

She had even greater doubts when, early the next morning, she calmly greeted André at her door, showed a properly civil front to offset his arrogance, and served him eggs Benedict on her good china, for old time's sake. Once again she prodded him on the matter of her money, confronting him with the falsified letter, engaging him in an argument perfectly designed to reveal every last detail of his devious scheme.

Her most grave doubts came, however, when the detective emerged from the bedroom and read André his rights. For an instant she was stirred by the stunned expression on his face, but when a mask of sheer ice replaced it she, too, hardened.

"None of this will stand up in a court of law," André seethed, coldly watching Tom, who had come to stand beside Serena.

It was the detective who answered. "Perhaps not the

letter. Any expert will discredit it. Now, as for these tapes, and a star witness . . ." All eyes turned toward Serena; at that moment she was terrified.

Tom, however, recognized her fear. Taking her hand he intertwined his fingers with hers and tucked her elbow through his as he stepped forward. "I don't think Serena will ever get to court." His gaze flicked warmly toward her before moving chillingly back to André. "My guess is that you'll make a plea."

André seemed unfazed. "I have nothing to confess."

"You may sing a different tune before long," Tom continued. "Larceny under false pretenses is one thing. Conspiracy to commit bribery on top of that is quite something else."

Serena wasn't the only one to stare at Tom. André paled. "What are you talking about?" he asked more quietly.

"Ann Carruthers. Edward Grant. I believe they're friends of yours. And I believe your schemes involve them, as well." André's concerned glance shot from Tom to the detective, then back. But Tom hadn't finished. "I know the Attorney General will appreciate your cooperation in bringing those aldermen to trial. If you do turn state's witness I'm sure we can settle this smaller matter quietly."

"*Smaller* matter?" Serena miraculously came to life. "What about my money, Tom? Have I lost it all? What about the satisfaction of seeing André pay for the agony he put me through? Where's the justice there?"

Turning, Tom put a forefinger against her lips. "Shhh." Then, glancing above her toward the detective, he snapped his head toward the door. Within a minute they were alone. "Listen, Serena, I'd like to go downtown with them. Just to make sure our interests are protected."

"When will you explain all this to me?" she asked, still bewildered and unable to accept that it was, in all probability, over.

"I'll be done later. You go to work. I'll stop by there on my way from the police station."

"Work? How can I think of work today . . . after this?"

"There's *Sweet Serenity*," he reminded her with a teasing smile. "It's your baby."

"But, Tom—"

"Shhh." Again he quieted her. This time, however, he reached for a folder that lay atop the recording equipment. "Here, take this with you. If you get a minute look at it. OK?" Before she was able to examine its contents Tom had kissed her and left.

10

This particular morning Serena's heart was no more in *Sweet Serenity* than her mind was on it. She opened the shop as usual, tending to the early dribble of customers only until Nancy arrived, when she took refuge in the back and opened the folder Tom had given her.

Anticipation of its contents made them no easier to examine. Even after sixteen years the pain of her father's downfall was intense. Yet what lay before her was no rehash of the newspaper clippings that had cut her so sharply once. Rather, Tom had offered his own file, his notes, his comments, his strategy, his raw data, and his personal log for her study.

For the first time Serena looked at the case from the standpoint of a less partial observer. For the first time she saw it through Tom's eyes. And, in the period of time it took her to go over each bit of information he'd gathered, each personal notation that had gone into the presentation of *his* case, she came to the conclusion that what he had maintained from the start of their reacquaintance

180

had been true. She might fault him for overenthusiasm, for making headlines of something that, given other circumstances, might have been buried on page forty-eight, but he had not been wrong in his indictment any more than the court had been wrong in its conviction. Her father had been guilty of embezzlement. For the first time she could truly accept that.

Closing the file at last, she came to a realization that had even more relevance to the present. Not only had Tom's findings been correct, but he had gone about reaching them in a faultless manner. His investigation had been a painstaking one, much slower and more cautious than she had previously imagined. His personal jottings revealed his own hesitation to print a word without what he felt was sufficient corroboration. Through it all came a very clear sense of conscience. With dawning respect for his commitment she wiped away the last of her doubts.

Suddenly it became imperative to speak with him. Her watch read eleven-thirty. The bustle of the lunch hour was approaching, but she couldn't wait. For everything that *Sweet Serenity* meant to her, Tom meant more. Leaving Nancy at the helm, she charged from the shop and took a cab to the police station.

The sergeant on duty was less than sympathetic. "Look, miss," he cajoled her, "*all* our business is urgent. Relax. Take it easy. We'll find him for you." With an indolence that made Serena want to scream the officer picked up the phone and made several calls before directing her down one corridor, up a set of stairs, to the left, then the right, then straight on ahead.

The miracle was that she found her way without a hitch. It helped that, on the last straightaway, Tom came running out to meet her. "What is it, Serena?" he cried in alarm, his hazel eyes as wide in fright as hers were in determination. "They said it was urgent. Is something wrong?"

"Can we talk somewhere?" she gasped, panting from

the exertion of racing to find him. "Some office, a closet—somewhere?"

Relieved to find her neither crying nor in the throes of a monumental headache Tom calmed down a bit. "Here, let's see." One by one he opened doors along the corridor, excusing his intrusion until at last he found a small cubicle with a table, two chairs, and total privacy. "This should do," he declared, following her in and closing the door behind them. "Now, what's this all about? What's happened?" He leaned back against the door, braced for a complication that was never to come.

For Serena faced him, smiled brightly, and rushed to wind her arms about his neck. "I love you. I just wanted to tell you that."

Incredulous, Tom studied the upturned face just inches below his. "What?"

"I love you."

The corners of his lips twitched in delight. "You ran all the way down here to tell me?"

"Yes. I love you."

"Say it again."

"I love you."

"You're sure?"

"Yes. I love you."

His arms grazed her hips as he raised them to lock about her waist. "No more doubts?"

"No."

"Go on." He waited for the chorus.

"I love you."

With a moan, he tightened his embrace, crushing her against him for a moment before lowering his head to kiss her. His lips parted hers; his tongue touched hers. And they both gasped at the shock that sent a burst of fire through them.

"Ahh . . . why here? Why here?" he rasped, trailing

his fingers down her spine to the small of her back. His subsequent pressing of her hips to his spoke of his instant arousal.

Serena's eyes held a hint of mischief. "Because I couldn't wait any longer. To tell you that. *And* to find out what's happening. Tell me about André's scheme."

He grinned. "You're a witch. Do you know that?"

She backed away from him and led him to the table, leaning against him when he perched on its edge. Her arms were still around his neck. She had no intention of letting go. "Tell me," she ordered in an urgent whisper.

Tom sighed. "André's theft of your money is only the tip of the iceberg. In the company of Alderpersons Carruthers and Grant the plan was to use municipal funds, supposedly invested in bonds, for reinvestment in the speculative deals he mentioned to you. In exchange for his use of the money André was giving healthy kickbacks to the other two, over and above his own killing."

"But he got nothing, or so he said."

"That was the catch. Had his speculation panned out he would easily have been able to replace not only your money, but the city's, without anyone being the wiser. Unfortunately, he's lost almost everything."

Serena had somehow been prepared for that. Her more immediate concern was elsewhere. "You knew about this before he talked, didn't you?" She eyed him askance.

"Yes, Serena. I did."

"That meeting that upset you so?"

"That was part of it, yes. I guess you want the whole story?"

"Well . . . ?"

"The Mayor contacted me shortly after I arrived in this area. He knew of my reputation as an investigative reporter and asked if I would keep an eye on something. He already suspected what was going on, but he needed evidence. This was one of those situations I mentioned hypothetically, where people in politics were involved and there was a question as to how deep the corruption ran. I was an outsider, a newcomer. It seemed a logical move."

"Have you gotten much?"

"Dribs and drabs. He was shrewd, for the most part. He slipped up when it came to you. He totally underestimated you." Tom smiled. *"He* didn't know about the fire in you."

"But he suspected you." She ignored his bait to rush on.

"I'm afraid my reputation preceded me, even though I retired from most investigative reporting several years ago. He was wary of me based on that reputation, but *our* relationship certainly didn't add to his peace of mind. And my knowing of your business involvement with him did nothing for *my* peace of mind. I feared you'd be put right in the middle and you were. Fortunately it's turned out for the best."

Serena nuzzled the firm skin of his neck. "You know, I was appalled at the insane desire for vengeance I felt before. That was an awakening! You were right about that, too—the sense of being victimized and having no faith that justice will be done. What will happen to André?"

"That's for the judge to decide. He's in the process of confessing everything, at his lawyer's recommendation, no less. The case against him is strong enough that, considering the public furor there will be when it all gets out, he'll be lucky to get away without serving hard time."

"He's ruined. It's a shame."

"It always is."

Their thoughts converged not on André, but on

Serena's father. At last they were in agreement and the matter was closed. With its closing, however, came the opening of a new, more immediate, yet far-reaching consideration.

"You'll marry me, won't you?" Tom asked softly.

"Is that what *you* want?" Her eyes glowed even through her concern.

"More than anything."

"But you've been through this once."

"No. It was totally different then. We were too young. We were totally ill-equipped to understand each other's needs, to fulfill them, and then, when it started to fall apart, to do anything about it."

"You said once that you feared involvement," she reminded him gently, wanting no stone left unturned.

"I was wrong then as you were wrong to let the ghost of the past haunt you, though I'm sure as hell glad it did. Otherwise you would have been long since snatched up before *I* arrived on the scene. I need you, Serena. I want you with me always." As she basked in the aura of his love he paused, waiting. "Well . . . will you . . . ?"

Her acceptance was whispered against his parted lips and was sealed with a kiss that stirred their depths to fan the smoldering fires. At that moment Serena knew that their love would conquer any obstacle that might fall in the path of their happiness. With Tom by her side she would find the strength to convince even her mother of its rightness. Once she was Tom's wife one *Sweet Serenity* would be more than enough to occupy any idle time he might leave her. And, when the time was right, her "new baby" would be a human one, with the promise of hazel eyes, good health and a smile that radiated from ear to ear.

"Let's get out of here," he growled, echoing her sentiments exactly. Totally wrapped up in each other, they headed home.

* * *

Her loose auburn waves brushed against his thigh as she made her way slowly over his body, savoring the taste of his flesh, exploring every last inch.

"Serena . . . Serena!" Reaching down Tom grasped her upper arms and hauled her abruptly along his length until she lay on top of him, eye to eye. "What do you think you're doing?" he asked half in fun, half in frustration. In truth he was driven nearly as wild now by the crush of her full breasts as he'd been by the sweet torment of her lips.

"I've changed my mind," she announced pertly.

"You've *what?*"

"Changed my mind."

Her smile and the sensuous way she slithered over him precluded true alarm. "About what?"

"You. You're no Apricot Brandy Cordial." She touched the tip of her tongue to his lips, then traced their manly line.

"Then what *am* I?" he murmured with the mingling of their breath.

She sighed happily. "A pure chocolate heart. Solid. Rich. Sweet. And endless."

Like our love, she thought, and nibbled some more.

Enjoy your own special time with Silhouette Romances.

Send for 6 books today— one is yours _free_!

Silhouette Romances take you into a special world of thrilling drama, tender passion, and romantic love. These are enthralling stories from your favorite romance authors—tales of fascinating men and women, set in exotic locations all over the world.

Convenient free home delivery. We'll send you six exciting Silhouette Romances to look over for 15 days. If you enjoy them as much as we think you will, pay the invoice enclosed with your trial shipment. **One book is yours free to keep.** Silhouette Romances are delivered right to your door with never a charge for postage or handling. There's no minimum number of books to buy, and you may cancel at any time.

Silhouette ❦ Romances

YOU'LL BE SWEPT AWAY
WITH SILHOUETTE DESIRE

$1.75 each

1 ☐ CORPORATE AFFAIR
James

2 ☐ LOVE'S SILVER WEB
Monet

3 ☐ WISE FOLLY
Clay

4 ☐ KISS AND TELL
Carey

5 ☐ WHEN LAST WE LOVED
Baker

6 ☐ A FRENCHMAN'S KISS
Mallory

7 ☐ NOT EVEN FOR LOVE
St. Claire

8 ☐ MAKE NO PROMISES
Dee

9 ☐ MOMENT IN TIME
Simms

10 ☐ WHENEVER I LOVE YOU
Smith

$1.95 each

11 ☐ VELVET TOUCH
James

12 ☐ THE COWBOY AND THE
LADY   Palmer

13 ☐ COME BACK, MY LOVE
Wallace

14 ☐ BLANKET OF STARS
Valley

15 ☐ SWEET BONDAGE
Vernon

16 ☐ DREAM COME TRUE
Major

17 ☐ OF PASSION BORN
Simms

18 ☐ SECOND HARVEST
Ross

19 ☐ LOVER IN PURSUIT
James

20 ☐ KING OF DIAMONDS
Allison

21 ☐ LOVE INTHE CHINA SEA
Baker

22 ☐ BITTERSWEET IN BERN
Durant

23 ☐ CONSTANT STRANGER
Sunshine

24 ☐ SHARED MOMENTS
Baxter

25 ☐ RENAISSANCE MAN
James

26 ☐ SEPTEMBER MORNING
Palmer

27 ☐ ON WINGS OF NIGHT
Conrad

28 ☐ PASSIONATE JOURNEY
Lovan

29 ☐ ENCHANTED DESERT
Michelle

30 ☐ PAST FORGETTING
Lind

31 ☐ RECKLESS PASSION
James

32 ☐ YESTERDAY'S DREAMS
Clay

33 ☐ PROMISE ME TOMORROW
Powers

34 ☐ SNOW SPIRIT
Milan

35 ☐ MEANT TO BE
Major

36 ☐ FIRES OF MEMORY
Summers

37 ☐ PRICE OF SURRENDER
James

38 ☐ SWEET SERENITY
Douglass

39 ☐ SHADOW OF BETRAYAL
Monet

40 ☐ GENTLE CONQUEST
Mallory

41 ☐ SEDUCTION BY DESIGN
St. Claire

42 ☐ ASK ME NO SECRETS
Stewart

**LOOK FOR _AFFAIR OF HONOR_
BY STEPHANIE JAMES
AVAILABLE IN MARCH AND
ONE NIGHT'S DECEPTION
BY KATHRYN MALLORY IN APRIL.**

SILHOUETTE DESIRE, Department SD/6
1230 Avenue of the Americas
New York, NY 10020

Please send me the books I have checked above. I am enclosing $_____
(please add 50¢ to cover postage and handling. NYS and NYC residents please add
appropriate sales tax.) Send check or money order—no cash or C.O.D.'s please.
Allow six weeks for delivery.

NAME _____

ADDRESS _____

CITY _____ STATE/ZIP _____

Silhouette Desire

Coming Next Month

Heart Over Mind by Sara Ann West

Brad Morrison was her boss and fiance, but Abby Kent found herself attracted to sculptor Travis Connery. Alone with Travis in New Mexico Abby was unable to resist his passionate persuasion.

A Wild, Sweet Magic by Suzanne Simms

He was too smooth, too rich, too handsome—the perfect target for cartoonist Kit Sinclair's wicked pen. But tycoon James Steele struck back, igniting a wild passion between them.

Experiment In Love by Rita Clay

Writer Victoria Brown was hoping to find a good story by advertising through a dating service. How could she know that Kurt Morgan had exactly the same idea?

Her Golden Eyes by Sara Chance

Tawny Summer McAllister was a born sailor, but from the moment Brandon Marshall stepped on board she was swept away by a wave of desire that engulfed them both.

Silver Promises by Suzanne Michelle

When TV newswoman Miranda Bowen met marine biologist Julian Hunter, she knew there was something special between them . . . something no ocean could keep apart.

Dream Of The West by Nora Powers

Melinda Adams was stunned when Cal, the rugged cowboy who had pursued her, turned out to be art collector Colin Marsden who remained aloof . . . with only his eyes betraying his desire.

Get 6 new Silhouette Special Editions every month for a 15–day FREE trial!

Free Home Delivery, Free Previews, Free Bonus Books. Silhouette Special Editions are a new kind of romance novel. These are big, powerful stories that will capture your imagination. They're longer, with fully developed characters and intricate plots that will hold you spellbound from the first page to the very last.

Each month we will send you six exciting *new* Silhouette Special Editions, just as soon as they are published. If you enjoy them as much as we think you will, pay the invoice enclosed with your shipment. **They're delivered right to your door with never a charge for postage or handling, and there's no obligation to buy anything at any time.** To start receiving Silhouette Special Editions regularly, mail the coupon below today.

Silhouette Special Edition

READERS' COMMENTS ON SILHOUETTE DESIRES

"Thank you for Silhouette Desires. They are the best thing that has happened to the bookshelves in a long time."
— V.W.*, Knoxville, TN

"Silhouette Desires—wonderful, fantastic—the best romance around."
— H.T.*, Margate, N.J.

"As a writer as well as a reader of romantic fiction, I found DESIREs most refreshingly realistic—and definitely as magical as the love captured on their pages."
— C.M.*, Silver Lake, N.Y.

*names available on request